The Girl *and* *the* Stolen Fiddle

The Girl *and*
the Stolen Fiddle

STEPHANIE JULIA GIBSON

RESOURCE *Publications* • Eugene, Oregon

THE GIRL AND THE STOLEN FIDDLE

Resource Publications
An Imprint of Wipf and Stock Publishers
199 W. 8th Ave., Suite 3
Eugene, OR 97401

www.wipfandstock.com

PAPERBACK ISBN: 978-1-6667-3179-8
HARDCOVER ISBN: 978-1-6667-2471-4
EBOOK ISBN: 978-1-6667-2472-1

MARCH 10, 2022 9:04 AM

To Mom and Dad
For getting me started
To Hope
For reading and laughing in between
To Ethan
For not letting me quit

CHAPTER 1

"GET YOUR HANDS OFF THAT!" Mrs. Aidan Odessa sat bolt upright in the sterile bed. Her hair and skin had the same starched crispness about them as the sheets. "Put it back," she bellowed. "Put it back this instant."

My left hand lay flat on the cold tile floor; my right hand grasped the perfect neck of the violin.

"I don't know what this world is coming to." Her eyebrows came together like thunderclouds. "People think they can waltz in and stick their noses anywhere they please."

I'm not sure why I took the instrument from its place on the shelf. I had never rifled through any of the residents' belongings before, and if Mrs. Aidan Odessa hadn't been sound asleep, I would have kept to the standard laundry rounds. Mrs. Odessa was still castigating, but my eyes dropped to the instrument resting in my hand. The dark wood was as smooth as a song. Silver strings lay over an ebony neck. Absolutely gorgeous—but it was the lack of a bow that first caught my attention. This beauty had no way to be played.

I meant to only take a quick peek. I had gingerly raised the fiddle from its case—not a bow in sight. I turned it over in my hand and admired the polished wooden surface. It was carved from a single piece of wood—a mark of high craftsmanship. I was thinking to myself what an excellent tone it should have when Mrs.

Aidan Odessa's shrill voice startled me, and I fell, fiddle in hand, to the floor.

"Young lady, this may be a nursing home, but that doesn't mean you can disregard a person's privacy."

I nodded, trying to look repentant. *I wonder how much trouble I will get into for this. Hopefully, just the standard lecture from Aunt Milly.*

I now pushed myself up and stood to face Mrs. Aidan Odessa directly. "I'm sorry, ma'am, would you like me to tune it up for you?"

"Get out! Out!" She lobbed a pillow at my head and began reaching for more ammo.

I ducked and hurriedly re-shelved the fiddle and ran into the hall, making sure I was out of sight. A pen clattered out the door behind me. She was still muttering as I snuck away. *Whoever said, 'it is better to ask forgiveness than permission' has never met Mrs. Aidan Odessa.*

I shuffled the tired old laundry cart into the next dingy room. Most of the residents here did not bother with the overhead light. Bits of sunlight squeezed through thickly curtained windows, but the result was only more shadows draping across the dungeon-like chambers. Rainy days were unbearable.

The first bed was empty. The blankets of bed number two rose and fell to gentle snoring. With one swoop, I gathered up bed number one's dirty laundry. *I'll never get used to that smell.* I tried to take my mind off my task. *Perhaps Mrs. Odessa had been in an orchestra in her sprier years. Maybe she had some forgotten fame and played for wealthy families—people do that. She was probably a bluegrasser.* I smirked at the image of Odessa in overalls playing "Turkey in the Straw."

The laundry cart crashed a little too hard into bed number two. I lunged forward, and my hands clenched the plastic handle. The blanket continued its steady snore—up, down, up. I let out a sigh of relief. "Good thing nobody has any hearing around this place." I backed the cart out the door and started into the next room.

"Melinda, can I speak to you for a moment?

How'd she find out so fast? "Be right there, Aunt Milly." I let the laundry cart roll into the hall and collide with the wall—leaving a dark gray streak. I winced. *I hope Aunt Milly didn't see that.*

"My office, please."

I sighed. In-the-office lectures were always the worst.

"Melinda. How many times have I told you to be respectful of the residents here?" My aunt's southern draw was thicker than anyone around here, and nothing was more important to her than manners and respecting your elders.

"I wasn't—"

"You were invading Mrs. Odessa's privacy."

"Aunt Milly, you *know* how she is."

"I *know* how you are." Aunt Milly's eyes were stern, but she wouldn't stay mad at me for long.

"I will try to do better." I turned to leave.

"Have a seat, Melinda."

"I understand, Aunt Milly; I'll respect the old lady's privacy from now on."

Aunt Milly didn't look up but pointed to the chair.

I groaned and slouched into the overstuffed armchair by the door.

"This is a perfect example of what we need to discuss. I've tried to be patient with you, but you are pushing your luck."

This was going to be a much longer lecture than I had anticipated.

"I understand this is a temporary job to get you through school," Aunt Milly said, "but let me tell you right now, your disregard for procedure and disrespect of this establishment will not get you anywhere in life."

"Aunt Milly, most of the regulations are a bunch of pointless hoops to jump through."

"The rules are there for a reason. Even if you don't know that reason, you will respect them."

"I follow the rules!"

Aunt Milly gave me *the* look.

I shrugged. "Unless they are stupid rules."

"It is more than that. You need to get out of your own world and start thinking about others a little more. That is what I have been trying to get across to you for years."

She had said it for years, alright. I've been told a billion times not to complain. In my mother's words: "Not everyone gets a job handed to them every year." It's true. It was nice to have a job any time I had a break from school, but I don't get paid nearly enough to revoke my right to complain. The only way to get through is to spice things up.

"Well?" Aunt Milly stared at me expectantly.

"Gotcha, by the book from now on."

She squinted at me suspiciously. "Good, because child, this is your final warning: one more incident out of you, and we're going to discuss if you get to keep this job."

I raised my eyebrows, but I wasn't concerned. Aunt Milly would never fire me. "It won't happen again," I said as I stood to leave.

"And Melinda . . . "

I turned with a half-hearted attempt to keep the annoyance off my face.

"I want you to stay away from Mrs. Odessa. You've aggravated her to no end. I'm assigning the East Wing to Helen."

I waved my hand in acknowledgment and headed out the door.

CHAPTER 2

I TRIED FOR THE REST OF the week to stay under my aunt's radar. This job paid better than most, and I need the money. Everyone on my laundry route is a mystery. When I first got here, I made the mistake of asking the residents themselves about their stories. If an exciting story is buried under all the grandchildren's names and ages, it will take forever to uncover it, and by that time, I am way behind. So instead, I try to discover each person's life story myself. I occasionally ask questions, but most of the time, I make up a story for each one based on what I notice about them and what mementos they keep with them around the room.

I had been trying to unravel the mystery of Mrs. Odessa for some time now, but the fiddle incident and Aunt Milly's order put the investigation on hold. I made it through the entire week without disturbing her, but she piqued my curiosity. No matter what story my mind's eye tried to impose on her, there was never a good fit. No, Mrs. Aidan Odessa was one nut I couldn't crack.

"Melinda, do you have a second?"

I was crouching next to my laundry cart, counting soap bottles. "What do you need?" I asked, turning to face Everly, one of the CNAs. I planned to become a CNA by next summer, so I had befriended her in hopes that she would help me out.

"We got a lunch cart spill in the East Wing and an incident in room 501 again. Can you go help with the cleanup? It's a big one."

"On my way," I said, leaving the laundry cart parked in a doorway.

Jello and mashed potatoes mixed with split pea soup were splattered all over the walls and floor. It was easy to see why the janitor had called in reinforcements. Not only was it a colossal mess, but we also had to keep the residents from coming through the hall. If anyone slipped and fell, we would have a much bigger problem on our hands. I grabbed a mop and got to work, reaching into the entryways of a couple of rooms to mop up the mess.

"Alright, I think we need to wipe down that last door."

"I can get it, Dan," I said, dunking a rag into the soapy water.

"Thanks for your help, Melinda."

"Anytime. Say hi to your mom for me." The last door had a few splatters on it, and I quickly wiped them clean. I was turning to go when a familiar voice spoke.

"*You* are the hooligan who nearly destroyed my violin."

Odessa. She had lowered the book she was reading and was eyeing me. I found it strange how much Mrs. Aidan Odessa read. Most of the residents' eyesight was failing at best, yet Mrs. Odessa always had a book in hand, and she never wore reading glasses.

"Yes, that was me." I attempted a smile at the old lady, but her face remained solemn. She pushed back her soft, snow-white hair that rested gracefully on her shoulders. The silence sent me into a nervous scramble for words. "I am sorry about that. I was rude."

"Indeed, you were," she said matter-of-factly.

Huh. I like this lady. "It's beautiful."

Mrs. Odessa peered over at the closed case, which housed the violin. "Mmm," she said shortly. She sat staunchly waiting for me to leave, but my curiosity got the better of me.

"Do you still play?"

"No."

"Ah."

"My laundry is right over there, behind that chair," she pointed to the corner, "Mind you, touch nothing else on the way."

I tossed my black ponytail behind my shoulder. "Yes, Ma'am."

Mrs. Odessa sat quietly, watching as I loaded the laundry onto the cart. "Well, you have a lovely day, Mrs. Odessa. Sorry again about the fidd-err violin."

She returned to her book, and she did not look in my direction again. *How can she read in that light? She must be at least 90 years old.*

CHAPTER 3

C HAOS IS MY FAVORITE WORD. Chaos is opening the door to my home and seeing the twins racing around the house. Kyle holds a wooden sword in one hand and attempts to keep his pirate hat on his head with his other hand as Kayla chases him around the coffee table with an eye patch stretched across her face. It is listening to Robin playing her scales up and down the piano as the smell of spaghetti and freshly fried zucchini wafts through the air. Chaos is Mom calling out, "Hello!" before the door slams shut. It's Ian nearly running into Daniel as they both set plates on our long wooden table; it is Dad opening the basement door with his elbows as he brings in some mason jars full of green beans from the pantry. This is chaos, and it is my favorite word.

I set my keys on the counter and grabbed a handful of spoons.

"All that work in the garden this summer sure paid off." Dad set the canned green beans on the counter.

"It better have after all the sweat and sunburn," I said under my breath. I jostled Kyle's hair as he ran past to show dad some new scientific discovery from the backyard.

"Alright!" Dad called, "Everyone to the table." Everyone claimed their seats in a minor uproar. There ain't nothing in this world like a country home-cooked dinner. Especially when the meal included garden goods, and Mom was the cook.

"Everyone, close your eyes and bow your heads," Dad directed and began to thank God for the food. I never closed my eyes or bowed my head during prayer. My family was a church family, and church was another place with a bunch of pointless rules. I would know. If the church doors were open, my family was lined up in the pew. The thing is, church is as flawed as any other place. People ruin everything, I guess. There are unwritten rules like close your eyes to pray, shake hands, and don't sing too loudly. I've never read any of those in the Bible. You even learn what I call Christianese—the art of talking churchy. You'll hear phrases like "I had a mountaintop experience" or "Please pray for traveling mercies." Those who are fluent may even slip in a "Let's enjoy the blessed fellowship of believers at the potluck today." Translation: let's eat.

" . . . Amen"

Everyone started grabbing steaming bowls of food.

"I'm telling you, being the youngest child is rough," Kyle said as he slurped up a forkful of spaghetti."

"You're a twin!" Daniel interjected. "That doesn't even count as the youngest."

"Kayla is five minutes and sixty-two seconds older than me."

Daniel rolled his eyes. "Will you think about what you said?"

I spooned a pile of zucchini onto my plate. "I don't know what y'all talking about. The oldest has it the worst."

"It is an indisputable fact that the middle child receives less attention and gets blamed for everything," Ian said.

Mom shook her head. "Y'all—"

I said, "The oldest child is the guinea pig."

"Melinda, you were not a guinea pig!"

"Mom, you have to admit, parents are the toughest on the oldest child."

"You're saying that because you got in trouble the most," Robin said, "I'm second-oldest, and I didn't get in trouble nearly as much as you."

"Because I *paved* the way for you."

"Yeah, right. Remember when you convinced Ian and me to have a mud fight with you in the front yard?"

"A brilliant idea," I said, smiling.

Ian laughed, "Yeah, except dad was trying to grow grass in our mud pie of a yard."

Dad raised his eyebrows in mock concern.

I nodded at him. "All in the name of good fun."

Mom shook her head. "I still have a picture of that day. You all were covered—except your eyes and big smiles."

"Humph, I don't remember you thinking it was cute."

"Yes, I did. I just didn't want you to do it again."

"Would you pass the bread, please?" Kyle asked impatiently.

"Remember that time Melinda pulled one over on the ice cream lady?"

I elbowed Daniel. "I was only in second grade."

"Plenty old enough to know that a penny wasn't seventy-five cents."

I sighed, "Poor lady. She sold me three penny ice cream cones before Mom figured out what I was up to."

"See?" Kyle said between bites. "At least you got away with stuff. I can't get away with nothing."

Dad laughed. "You all are good kids. We are thankful for each one of you."

Mom nodded. "Yes, a rough and tumble crew we have, but y'all are good kids." I caught her eye as she said this. Her eyes were always smiling.

I loved my family, but being in a large family meant there was never much to spare. That is why I wanted to get a high-end job someday. I want to go out and get a fancy meal whenever I want without breaking the bank. Of course, I'd also like to help my family out as well. I know my parents sacrificed a lot for us. I wanted a different life for myself, but I also wanted to give back to them.

These are the kinds of thoughts I have on my drive to work every morning. Early mornings were not my prime time. It was the only time I didn't turn up the music. The door whooshed open as I made my way groggily to the laundry room. Nothing in this world is more tedious than folding laundry. I started pulling sheets out of the dryer. Supposedly, Mrs. Odessa is loaded. The lady is the only resident in Fairview with a room to herself. *Did she make her money playing the fiddle? Maybe she'll give me some tips.* She was such an intriguing person, and I found myself again wandering through her door by the end of the day. It was after hours, so Aunt Milly shouldn't have any problem with that.

"Did I say come in?" The voice was flat and smooth.

Well, this is new. Mrs. Aidan Odessa was sitting straight up in bed. She had the thin white sheet pulled up under her armpits, and her hands were folded calmly on her lap.

Aunt Milly's threat flashed through my mind, and I slid my tongue over my bottom lip, "I'm sorry."

"Don't apologize," she said. "Make it right."

I cocked my head, forced back the impulse to roll my eyes, and slowly backed the cart into the hall. I glanced around to make sure Aunt Milly wasn't anywhere nearby. Then, feeling the ridiculousness of it all, I gently rapped my knuckles on the hallowed door and raised my eyebrows expectantly.

The smooth voice calmly asked, "Who is it?"

I frowned and cleared my throat, "Laundry."

No answer.

"May I come in?"

"Come."

"Someone already collected my laundry," she watched my every move, "and you do not have any clean laundry with you."

"Oh, I, I'm sorry, I guess, I'll, I'll go," I started walking back out the door.

"What is your name, girl?"

I turned around slowly. "Melinda Newman, ma'am."

"Hm."

Someone was talking in the hallway. *Gotta go.*

Mrs. Odessa called from behind me, "You have spunk, Melinda Newman." I raised my hand to wave, but Mrs. Aidan Odessa was no longer looking at me. Her eyes stayed fixated on the violin. The wrinkles around her mouth and eyes suggested an ever-present smile. Those smiles were long forgotten now.

"Have a good day, Mrs. Odessa," I whispered and slipped into the hall.

CHAPTER 4

O VER THE NEXT SEVERAL DAYS, I returned to room 301 whenever I got the chance. Mrs. Odessa and I were not friends, and we never would be, but she became my favorite stop. She never told me anything about herself. She never said much, except each time I turned to leave, she would send me off with a quiet, "You have spunk, Melinda Newman."

Between armfuls of clothes, I told her all about my crazy family, my dreams of being a doctor, and my secret love of deep-fried pickles. Mrs. Aidan Odessa never took her hard stare off me, except for the rare occasion when I observed her gaze resting on the violin.

"Aunt Milly always insists I take a week off before school starts. 'Not good for anyone to work too hard.'" I stuck my chest out in my best Aunt Milly impression and laughed at myself. Mine was the only laughter, but I didn't mind.

Mrs. Odessa didn't acknowledge me. She had not moved her eyes off the fiddle this morning.

"Hopefully, next summer, I can become a CNA. It is a major step up from laundry lady and only takes a four-week class—"

"You talk a lot for one with such little experience."

I faced her brazenly. "And you talk very little for one with so much experience."

"The wiser you are, the less you talk."

"Well," I said, "that is a shame. Maybe that is why the world is the way it is—the wise refusing to share their wisdom."

"Wisdom is rarely shared by talking about it." Odessa's eyes turned once more to the shelved violin. "Experience produces wisdom."

I returned to place the folded shirts into the drawer. "How did you end up here, Mrs. Odessa?"

A deep sigh came from behind me. "I see myself in you, Melinda. Although it was ages ago, I, too, had the world figured out."

"I don't claim to have everything figured out."

"Your actions speak louder than your words," Odessa said as she reached for her book and began flipping to her spot.

"You have to be determined if you want to get anywhere in this world." Odessa was not listening to me now, but I continued, "I mean, you know that. You had to be determined to make all your money." I glanced up to see if I would get a response, but she remained quiet, and sadness clouded her face.

"Laundry," a gentle voice said. "Melinda? Aren't you—"

"Helen, I have this covered," I said, attempting a pleasant smile.

"But didn't your—"

"As you can see, I have patched things up."

Helen glanced at Mrs. Odessa, who calmly nodded and said, "The laundry has already been taken care of here. It would be prudent for you to move on to your next room. Do not be a time-waster."

"We are returning to normal routes, Helen," I said. "It's alright."

Helen shook her head and rolled into the hall. "Whatever you say."

CHAPTER 5

F ROM THAT DAY FORWARD, WHENEVER I made a stop in Mrs. Odessa's room, I would fold the clothes a little slower and gather the hamper with more care. Mrs. Aidan Odessa was the strangest person I'd ever met. She had learned everything about me by this time—only two weeks until Christmas—and I didn't know anything about her. Whenever I tried to discover anything about her, she would answer as vaguely as possible.

"Where have you traveled?" I would ask.

"Oh, just about everywhere," she answered.

"Any family?"

"All no accounts," she would sigh.

"What did you do for a living?"

"Oh, a little bit of this, and a whole lot of that."

"Any children?"

"Not one," she said.

"Where did you get your fiddle?"

And on this question, she was silent.

Just when I accepted that I would never learn any details about her, she asked, "Do you know how old I am?"

I have often tried to estimate Mrs. Odessa's age. Her snow-white hair and map of wrinkles made her seem timeworn and frail, yet she was spirited, and her mind was as sharp as her eyes. I tossed the last bit of laundry onto the cart. "Not a day over sixteen." Not even a spark of amusement lit in her eyes. She demanded a serious answer. "I wouldn't have a guess, Mrs. Odessa."

She straightened her thin, bony shoulders, and her face grew more serious than I had ever seen it. *Is she gonna cry?*

"Tomorrow is my two hundred and thirty-second birthday."

My first impulse was to laugh. I bit back my grin and managed to only let a breathy gasp escape. *Maybe this lady is not as sharp as I gave her credit for.* Her face was unsmiling. I shook my head. She believed with every fiber of her being that she, Mrs. Aidan Odessa, was over two centuries old. What was even more bizarre was as I stood there staring at her stony face and fiery eyes, I believed it, too.

Mrs. Odessa lifted her hand. She was shaking, not out of frailty, but as if she were angry. Her finger pointed to the violin. "It is because of this."

I tried to mirror her solemnness. "What? Is the fiddle like your life source?"

Mrs. Aidan Odessa said nothing, but her chin tilted down in a slow nod.

Craziness must be contagious. It rattled me that I had believed the old coot for half a minute. With all her reading and serious demeanor, I had not pegged Mrs. Aidan Odessa as the crazy type. I sighed; *what if—nah. Just another looney at Fairfield.* I didn't say goodbye; I rolled my cart out of the room. As I turned the corner, I let a giggle trickle out. However, my laughter was cut short by what was in front of me.

Aunt Milly was in the middle of the hall, hands on her hips, coming toward me.

I'm usually so careful. It would take some effort to talk my way out of this one.

"Melinda Jane Newman. Did I not give you express instructions to stay away from Mrs. Odessa?"

"You did, Aunt Milly, but if—"

"No, Melinda, you can't explain this away."

"If you will talk to her, you'll see that everything's smoothed over."

"Melinda, that is not the point. You ignored my instructions." Aunt Milly shook her head.

"Please, just go talk to her."

"This is hard for me to do; we are family after all, but your behavior is unacceptable. Go get your things."

"Aunt Milly?"

"Go get your things. You no longer have a job here."

"Wait, you're firing me?" I pushed the cart away, and it rolled into the wall. "Are you serious?"

"This is the last straw, Melinda. I'm sorry." She trudged down the hall.

"Aunt Milly, come on, talk to Odessa. You, you know I need this job!" She disappeared around the corner.

I kicked the cart, pushing it harder into the wall and leaving another mark. I bowed my head to my fist, trying to think of a way to fix this. *Odessa. I have to get her to talk to Aunt Milly for me. No, that won't work. Odessa is obviously crazy. Who knows what she would tell Aunt Milly.*

In a crazed impulse, I rush to the nurses' station. "Hey!" I motioned for the nurse to come over to where I was standing.

"Hey, Melinda, ready for the holidays?"

"Listen, I have a quick question."

"Yeah?"

"Room 301. Is she on any meds?"

"Melinda, you know I can't tell you—"

"Come on; I need to know for, for Milly. Any meds?"

The nurse sighed and then shrugged. "She doesn't get any. Well, she refuses them anyway. I think she is afraid of being found out."

"Found out?"

"I really shouldn't be telling you this, but her case is strange. No one seems to know anything about her."

"What do you mean?"

"Well, she has no birth certificate or records of any sort. I hear tell, she's been all over the world. They say she's rich, you know. Her bill is paid up in cash."

I tried not to let my face give away the butterflies in my stomach.

"I'm surprised you didn't know this already. Seems like your aunt would have told you. It was her call to let her stay here."

"What if she is a criminal or something?"

"Well, you know what they say: 'ignorance is bliss.' Well, that's the end of my shift; I'll see you tomorrow."

"Yeah." I stood rooted to the white tile as the nurse moseyed away. "Hey, um, you don't know how old she is, do you?"

The nurse shrugged. "Your guess is as good as mine, honey."

CHAPTER 6

"WHAT AM I GOING TO DO? What am I going to do?" I was driving around town—unwilling to go home. I still had a month of work left before school started again. I need the money for tuition. Mom and Dad would go ballistic when they found out I had gotten myself fired. "I have to go back." I swung the car around in a wild U-turn. *My only option is to talk to Odessa and get her to tell Aunt Milly that she enjoys my company. Odessa is crazy, but she is my only chance. I have to convince her to help. How to get on her good side?* "I need to stop by the bakery."

It wasn't anything fancy—a confetti cupcake and a flickering candle stuck down the middle. I snuck in the door, checking around for any signs of Aunt Milly. Then I slinked down the hallway to room 301. Mrs. Aidan Odessa was reading one of her books when I peeked in. "May I come in?"

If she was surprised by either me or the cupcake, her face did not say so. "Come."

I set the birthday peace offering on her nightstand. "So, two-thirty-two, huh?"

She picked up the cupcake and was about to blow out the flame. "Wait!" I said as I shut the door after one last glance down the halls. "You have to make a wish first."

She turned her stern gaze toward me.

I shrugged. "I don't make the rules."

Wax dribbled down the little blue candle, and the flame danced in her dark eyes. Then poof! It was gone. "Yes," she said, "two hundred thirty-two."

We sat. The second hand was as loud as a grandfather clock at midnight. Would it break the spell that kept me here?

Mrs. Aidan Odessa reached out and clasped my hand. It was not a tender gesture but instead had an urgency about it. "Do you believe me?"

" . . . Yes." I did not. Mrs. Aidan Odessa's eyes pierced through me, but the urgency in her demeanor did not lessen. She released my hand and sat back. "I need you to do something for me, Melinda." Her hand now guided my eyes to the fiddle. "Everything depends on it."

A strange thing for a 200-something-year-old to say.

"Sit."

"Listen, I need a favor—"

"Sit." She did not raise her voice or turn her eyes away from the violin. "You see that instrument there."

Had she forgotten my history with her precious fiddle? This conversation did not bode well for my hopes of her putting in a good word with Aunt Milly.

"It is not mine." She abruptly turned back to me.

I raised my eyebrows, unsure of what she would say next. Finally, I ventured, "Well, whose is it?"

"It is stolen."

"Stolen? By who? By you?"

Odessa nodded slowly.

"Oh." I searched for words. "Is it . . . valuable?"

"It must be returned. It is the only way I can make things right, and I . . . " her voice broke, " . . . can be in peace."

I swallowed hard—my head was spinning. "I don't understand. What does this have to do with me?" I mentally added "consorting with criminals" to my list of misdeeds.

"I need you to return it to its rightful place. I will cover all of your expenses."

Mrs. Aidan Odessa was not asking me to do this for her—she was ordering me to. However, the all-expenses-covered part piqued my interest, and I waited for her to explain.

"Here." She reached into her nightstand drawer and pulled out a small box. She opened it, brought out a piece of paper, and handed it to me.

"Airplane tickets!" I gasped, "to Switzerland? Where—how did you get these?"

"That isn't important now," she said, pulling out another piece of paper from the drawer.

I had never been out of the United States of America in my whole life—not even to Canada. "I don't know what you think I am going to do, but I don't want to be involved in this." My outburst did not move Mrs. Aidan Odessa.

"Now," she said, " you must promise to do exactly as I say. If you do not, you will never return home." My head snapped up. *Is she threatening me?* Her face was set in her usual matter-of-fact manner.

"I haven't agreed to this." I meant to match her commanding tone, but it had come out as a whisper.

She eyed me—as if measuring me against some unknown standard. Then her face brightened, and the gentlest look I had ever seen settled on her face. "But you will go," she said simply.

She's right.

"Take down the violin."

"Odessa—"

"Bring it to me," she demanded.

I got up slowly and carefully took the fiddle down from the shelf, this time cradling it like a baby. My fingers lay across the cold metal strings. "Is there no bow?" I asked.

"No," was the sharp reply. Mrs. Aidan Odessa reached into the box again and pulled out an envelope. "Take this. It should be plenty for your trip."

I took the envelope and peeked inside. It was packed full of more money than I had ever dreamt of seeing in my life.

CHAPTER 6

"My life's savings. This is only half of it. You will receive the rest when you return. I will not need it anymore if you are successful."

I stared open mouthed at the stack of money in my hands.

"Remember," Mrs. Aidan Odessa said earnestly, "When you reach the curtained door, you must speak to no one. No one can see you. Above all, you must *touch nothing*. Stick to the job—take the violin to the music arena behind the falls and get out as quickly as possible. The longer you stay, the worse it will be for you. It's all detailed here." She placed the piece of paper in my hand.

I was still staring at the money. "Mrs. Odessa, is this 'job,' well, I mean, is this legal?"

Her face saddened. "Child, this is a place that does not abide by government law or nations. Nothing you do will land you in jail," she cleared her throat and drew her eyebrows together, "but it is dangerous. Do not enter this task lightly."

I bit my lip. *Clearly, I am going on a pointless trip for a woman who has lost her mind. Or maybe I am losing my mind.* I squeezed the wad of cash in my hand. *It would solve all my problems. Plus, a free trip to Switzerland.*

"Your plane leaves tomorrow."

"But I haven't even told—"

"You will not need to pack much. Just enough for the travel days."

"But I will be gone at least a week!"

She nodded at the door. "Safe journey. Make sure you are successful."

I plodded forward in a stupor with the ticket, the money, and the note in one hand, and the cased violin swinging by my side. I glanced back over my shoulder, and Odessa was still watching me with her solemn gaze. "Goodbye, Mrs. Aidan Odessa." I am not sure if the words made it out of my throat. Whether or not they did, there was no reply.

CHAPTER 7

I ROLLED INTO OUR DRIVEWAY AND sat staring at the front door. Mom was home already. I had driven around town for the last two hours to not raise suspicions about why I was returning home early. The money and the plane tickets sat beside me on the passenger's seat, and the fiddle rested in its coffin-like case on the back seat. I was in a lot of trouble.

Aunt Milly fired me. I reached for the envelope. *That beautiful money. I can't go to Switzerland, can I? I have to return it. Odessa would report that I stole the money if I didn't do what she asked. How can I possibly do what she asked? So what? I go to Switzerland, drop off the fiddle, and bam! I'm rich.* I clenched the envelope. *Rich.*

I slowly opened the car door and went toward the house. I had no plan. Mom was singing softly and washing the dishes.

"Oh, hi, hon. Your dad is bringing up some boxes from the basement; why don't you go help him."

"Um, I actually needed to talk to you both about something."

"Hmmm? What's that?"

"That should be the last box," Dad said, coming through the door.

Mom strolled over to me and motioned Dad to come over. "Melinda wants to tell us something."

Dad came over, brushing the basement grime from his hands.

"Yeah. Well, okay," I tried desperately to think how to phrase this. "I, um, happened to find ah—an amazing opportunity." I tried to sound enthused.

"What amazing opportunity would that be?" Dad asked.

Well, I want to take the rest of my winter break and do something a little spontaneous. Go on a trip."

"For the rest of your break?" Mom started, "What about your work?"

"You know, I talked to Aunt Milly. It is such a great opportunity for me—well, she, she said not to come back to work."

Mom's forehead wrinkled. "Milly is encouraging this? She knows how important this job is for your education."

"You know we can't help with tuition," Dad said.

"Well, see, there it is. I think you both will be pleased. I have the opportunity to go on an all-expense-paid trip to . . . Switzerland!"

"Melinda, you have no experience traveling," Mom said. The concern was growing on her face.

"I will be fine. You know, I'll figure it out."

A loud "Humph!" came from Dad.

"Would you be traveling with a group? Is this through your school?" Mom questioned.

"No, it's a solo trip."

"No," Dad said, standing up and walking back toward the dusty boxes.

"Excuse me, no?" I said, taken aback.

"Traveling that far by yourself isn't safe, especially for you who has never been out of the country. And who exactly is paying for this solo trip?" Dad questioned.

I stood, the irritation mounting in my voice. "You know, I, I, I'm not asking your permission."

"I don't like the sound of this 'all-expense-paid solo trip.'" Dad said.

"Melinda, are you going to be gone for Christmas? Don't you want to stay for Christmas?"

"We'll talk about this more later." Dad trudged out of the room.

Mom patted my arm. "You will be glad you stayed for Christmas."

I shook my head and slipped by her and out the door. I paced around in the driveway, stopping every few seconds to stare through the window at the money.

The following day, I rolled out of bed, put on my work clothes, and crept down the stairs and out the door.

Going to Switzerland. Don't worry. Be back for Christmas.
Love,
Melinda

I taped the note to the front door. "If I make it back alive, I am so dead."

CHAPTER 8

A MAN IN A THICK COAT knocked into my shoulder as he rushed by. "Verzeihung," he coughed. I pulled my scarf up over my nose and held my bag tightly as I shuffled forward toward the street, trying to avoid the sidewalk bustle. I raised a mittened hand to hail a taxi for the first time in my life. The town Mrs. Aidan Odessa was sending me to was two hours away from the airport. I held tightly with mittened hands to the scribbled directions Mrs. Odessa had given me. Finally, a taxi stopped. I scrambled in, thankful to be out of the wind, and sat shivering in the back seat, rubbing my bare hands together to regain some warmth.

"Wohin?" the sturdy driver questioned.

I swallowed back the mounting panic. "I'm sorry, uh, do you speak English?"

"You put your bags in zee seat and tell me vere you vould like to goh."

"Oh, thank you. Andermatt, please?"

"Jah, but it vill kost you a good 'andful of francs."

"I know, but I need to get there fast."

"Vell, ve're off sen!"

The Southern Alps framed the roadway. I wiped away the window fog with my sleeve. The sky was overcast, but the snow caps still shone. I still had my directions clenched between my gloves.

"Miss?" The taxi driver eyed me in the rearview mirror. "I am looking for a man named Mr. Jay Swartzentruber. I know it's a long shot, but any chance you know where he lives?"

The taxi driver laughed heartily. "Zere are dozens ov Swartzentrubers in zese parts."

"He is old, like really old."

The woman frowned, and when she spoke, it was with husky suspicion in her voice. "How did you find out about olt Swartzentruber?"

"You know him?" I wasn't sure if I was relieved or more stressed that someone else confirmed Odessa's madness.

"Vell, I'd say everyone has heard ov him. Zey say he's been around as long as zese hills."

"Do you know how to find him?"

"Not easy to find. No one knows vere he lives. No one has seen him for years. Dead, I vager."

"Dead!" My breath fogged the cab window. "Is there anyone who might know more about him?"

The thick-boned taxi driver shrugged.

I read over the directions for the hundredth time:

1. Find Mr. Jay Swartzentruber. He will lead you to the vine-curtained door.

2. Enter with nothing except the violin.

3. Do not let anyone see you.

4. Keep out of the light.

5. Place the violin behind the waterfall.

Well, I guess if I can't complete the first step, I'll finish the rest of my vacation in peace. I will tell Mrs. Odessa I did my best, but I can't do nothing about the man dying.

"I know who can help you find olt Swartzentruber—if he exists."

My newfound relief vanished.

"You finden my friend Mavis. She klaimed to know him vell. If anyone knows vere to find zee olt boy, it's Mavis."

"Alright, um, take me to Mavis . . . um, please."

"Du hast es!"

To my surprise, the taxi driver wheeled around, nearly doing a donut in the snow, and backtracked down the road we had traveled down. I adjusted my jacket, blew a tuft of hair out of my face, and said, "Where does Mavis live exactly?"

"In town. It is a schame you got me to drive you so far for nothink. But I vill shtill have to charge zee usual fee—you understanden?"

"Right." *This Mavis better be worth it.*

The taxi driver stopped in front of a small townhouse. I put my feet on the icy walk and grudgingly paid the taxi driver far more francs than this trip had been worth.

"Enjoy your shtay in Switzerland!" She said, crumpling the cash in her gloved hand.

I walked up to the small porch and rang the doorbell. I waited for the sound of footsteps, but none approached. I rang the bell again for good measure. No one came to the door. *What now? Of course, the taxi is out of sight. Maybe I should check into hotels for the night.*

"Haaaaalloo there!"

The neighbor lady was waving at me. "Mavis is at zee schop!" She gestured up the sidewalk to the little town, two blocks away.

I squinted at her. "What shop?"

"Zee grocers," the woman said, "Lidl's."

I shift my bag to my left shoulder. "Well, I guess I'll wait for her here," I said, lowing myself to the snow-dusted step.

"You vill be vaiting a vile." The woman bellowed, "You know how Mavis is."

"I haven't met her."

"Oh! You vill know her ven you see her!" The woman did not seem concerned that she was sending a stranger to find her neighbor. "You looken for her bright red hair." I would rather find Mavis than continue this yelling match. I waved my thanks and walked down the sidewalk.

The whoosh of warm air welcomed me into the small store. A drum of words, untranslatable to my American brain, bustled around me. I grabbed a shopping basket to blend in and milled around, looking for any sign of red hair.

Then it was there—bright, bouncy, and oh-so-red. Even if everyone in Switzerland had been a redhead, there would have been no doubt in my mind that this was Mavis. She was wearing a bright blue snow puffer, and her cheeks were flushed brighter than her hair. I would have pegged her for a rodeo gal straight out of Texas if not for her thick accent. She was talking a mile a minute to anyone who would listen. I approached her slowly. "Mavis?"

"Ja? Kann ich Dir helfen?" The bouncy woman swirled around in my direction and was a little taken aback when she found me standing there. "Ja? Was ist das, kind?"

I sucked air through my teeth—the woman's perfume was overwhelming. "Do you speak English?"

"Nein Englisch, Sprichst du Deutsch?"

I shook my head. "Nothing is going to be straightforward today."

"Was sagst du Kind?" The woman gestured to herself, "Brauchst du mich?"

"Mr. Swartzentruber?" I absently gestured to my face, stroking my chin like a beard. "Do you know him?"

"Alt Swartzentruber?"

I nodded emphatically.

Mavis pulled a box of crackers off the shelf and nodded to herself. She pointed at me. "Amerika?"

"Yes, America." I pulled Odessa's note out of my pocket. "His friend asked me to find him."

The woman gently took the note from my hand and studied the wrinkled lines. "Jay." She pointed to the words. "Jay Swartzentruber." Then she walked away. She was leaving the store.

"Miss Mavis! Your buggy!" I sputtered, but she was not stopping. I tossed my shopping basket into her cart and hurried after her.

CHAPTER 8

I was following a wind-up toy. Mavis was about ten feet in front of me, and she did not turn around. *"Does she even know I'm back here?"* I bumped my way back into the cold—trying not to slip on the icy walkway. Mavis kept on trucking.

CHAPTER 9

I DROPPED THE FIDDLE CASE IN the snow and bent over, resting my hands on my knees, trying to catch my breath. Mavis had halted and turned to face me. Her cheeks were still wildly flushed, but other than that, she did not appear winded in the least. "I'm not fond of the taxi service around here, but I'd've gladly footed the bill," I puffed. Mavis had trudged expertly down this old snow-packed driveway that had led us into the wooded mountains. The town was still visible below.

Mavis pointed to a large oak tree. "Jay Swartzentruber," she said with exaggerated enunciation. Then she smiled at me, sandwiched my face between her thick, mittened hands, and kissed both my cheeks. I childishly rubbed the kisses off my face, and Mavis began her quick descent down the mountain.

"Wait! Where are you going?"

"Auf Wiedersehen, kind!" Mavis did not turn around but waved her hand.

"You're going to leave me here?" I glanced up to where she had pointed. No Jay Swartzentruber, not even a house. Nothing but a bunch of nature. I shook my head. *How much longer am I going to go along with this?* I took a lunging step forward. Mavis was still barely visible, plodding back to town. It wasn't too late to run after her.

I surveyed my surroundings once more. *Wait. Footprints. Footprints in the snow.* I pulled up to the top of a bank and nervously scanned the horizon—still no one around. I stretched to match the tracks to not leave fresh prints, but the violin combined with my many layers made it difficult to copy the treader's gate. I looked over my shoulder for any signs of someone following me. My eyes traced every tweet and crackle, but no signs of anything with snow boots. The tracks stopped abruptly about three feet from the old tree Mavis had pointed to. I stared at the gnarly trunk. All around was untouched powdery snow. "Ok," I said under my breath, "this is getting creepy."

"Well, I prefer eccentric," a voice with a crisp English accent said.

I let out a sharp shriek and fell backward. So much for stealth. I searched frantically for the speaker.

The voice was coming from above me, and there he was, like some sort of Peter Pan, standing on a rope ladder, lowering toward me. The ladder was attached to a pulley and was connected to the most elaborate treehouse I had ever seen. Even as I was looking straight at it, it took me a moment to see it. It was camouflaged well in the branches and snow. The man was now right above me. If I had enough sense to stand up, we would have been eye to eye. He was a short, scrawny man—completely bald. He extended his hand toward me. "Jay Swartzentruber, at your service."

CHAPTER 10

"DESSY SENT SOMEONE AT LAST!" Mr. Jay Swartzentruber had a massive voice for such a wiry man. It was as if someone set a bow to Odessa's fiddle, but a pipe organ played from its strings. From the inside, I would never have known this was a treehouse. Its tall ceilings were painted elegantly, and the polished hardwood floor shone in the soft winter light. Everything had a sort of posh yet extraordinarily mixed-up feel to it.

"Have a seat, have a seat!" the man exclaimed.

A lavish couch sat in front of a delicate stained-glass windowpane. I gingerly lowered myself onto it. The material was stiff, and the couch was overstuffed. Mr. Swartzentruber handed me a dainty teacup.

"So," His eyes were a pale blue which matched the winter sky, "You have the instrument?"

"Yes, I have it right here." I reached over to open the case.

"No, don't show me! It is better if I do not see."

I withdrew my hand and awkwardly crossed my ankles, trying to get comfortable.

"I suppose Aidan told you what is at stake?"

"No," I said, taking a sip of tea, "no, she didn't tell me much at all."

"Ah, just like the old girl. If we told you too much, it might scare you off entirely. Biscuit?"

I glanced up from my steaming cup. "No, thanks. So, you know Mrs. Aidan Odessa?"

"Know her? Ha! We grew up together! In fact, I was with Aidan when she, ah, acquired the instrument. Afterward, it was best for us to part ways to avoid suspicion. I haven't seen her since I was a lad. Of course, I've tried to contact her, but I only received this from her after all those years." He pulled out a faded envelope and handed it to me.

"Dearest Jay," I read, "I will send someone to return what was taken. Love, Aidan."

"Of course, it has been years since she wrote this, but obviously, it would take some time for her to find the person for the task." He squinted at me for a moment. "And it seems she has chosen." He did not seem altogether pleased by Odessa's choice.

"Did you steal it together? Is it valuable?"

Jay swirled his spoon in his teacup. "I must admit, it is Aidan who wishes to return the blasted thing." He ran a hand over his smooth head. "We ought to leave well enough alone."

"Won't there be some sort of reward?"

"The reward, if you succeed, is your life."

I blinked at him in stunned silence. He continued, "Honestly, I can't think why on earth Dessy would have picked you."

I set my cup on the windowsill. "I can do the job. Listen, I don't know what you think of me, but I can handle myself, and I don't know if you are trying to keep this fiddle for yourself or what, but it ain't gonna work."

"How old are you, girl?"

I set my jaw. "How old are you, Mr. Swartzentruber?"

He carefully put the note away in his shirt pocket. "Old enough to know it never ends well when I answer that question."

"Well," I said through my teeth, "I better follow the example of my elders."

"Look, young lady—"

"It's Melinda," I said in a low voice.

"I'm going to level with you. Aidan and I have a past we're not proud of, and while I believe it's best to let the past be the past,

Aidan has done all manner of risky business trying to put to rights the wrongs we committed in our youth." He tapped the lid of the fiddle case. "This here is the last piece." He took my still-brimming teacup to a small adjoining room, saying, "I enjoy the life I am living. Aidan was never content with anything." He came back into the room and leaned in the doorway. "I dare say, she must be paying you a substantial amount to take on this job."

"I'm sorry, do you have a bathroom?" I stood from the cumbersome couch.

"Yes, of course, through there."

I hesitated to leave the fiddle and my bag, but I didn't want to raise suspicion by taking everything to the bathroom. I closed the lavish door. The light poured through a smaller stained glass window, making a rainbow pattern across the sink. *I need to get out of here.* I flushed the toilet so as not to raise suspicion. I turned on the sink and stood watching the water swirl down the drain—marveling at the fact that this treehouse had such sophisticated plumbing. Then I stoically turned the doorknob and put on a pleasant smile. "Well, thank you for your help, but I really should go," I said, barely glancing in his direction.

He was already out the door and pulling at the ladder, "Of course, we must not waste any time."

I pulled my backpack over my right shoulder.

I reach down to pick up the hard-shelled violin case. *It's too light.* I shook my head, processing what had happened. *He took it.* Jay stood by the doorway, getting the rope ladder ready. I still held the case—my other hand balled into a fist. "Where did you put it?" I said, moving swiftly toward him.

He didn't reply but instead pulled the fiddle out from behind a curtain and rushed forward. The fiddle was in one hand, a ladder rung in the other. He smirked. "You think I'd ever be willing to give up all this?" He gestured to the grand set-up all around him, "If Aidan wants to appease her guilty conscience, that is all well and good, but I am happy with my arrangement." He swung onto the rope ladder. "It was delightful meeting you, Melinda."

I ran, and without hesitating, leaped onto the rope ladder. It was a shaky landing. One of my legs went straight through the ladder, but I managed to land on one foot, grabbing the ladder with my right hand and still gripping the fiddle case with my left. Jay was halfway down. I began swinging the empty case at the scoundrel's head.

Jay ducked to avoid the blows. I was too high to reach him. He started climbing down more rapidly as the ladder lowered, and I followed him, still swinging the case. We were about ten feet above the ground. Finally, I threw the case at his head. He reflexively let go of the ladder, grabbed his head, and fell hard into the snow. I jumped down after him and lunged to tear the fiddle from his hand.

He was much stronger than I expected him to be, and he leaped up with a grunt and expertly wrenched the violin out of my reach, and took off running in the opposite direction from the town road. Jay darted through the snow with ease. I pushed myself up and stumbled after him. An abandoned building made of stone and brick caught my eye. Thick vines covered an arched doorway, but I didn't see any other windows or openings as I glanced at it. Jay was leading me away from this tower, so of course, that is precisely where I determined to go. A curtained door—just as Odessa had said—it had to be it. *Violin first.* I plowed through the snow with renewed vigor. Jay was running towards a part sleigh, part snowmobile.

"Ha!" I pushed ahead. "Where has this baby been all day?" I was close enough to tag Jay's arm. He tossed the fiddle into the back seat of the contraption and swung himself behind the driver's wheel. The engine roared. As he pulled away, I grabbed the top rail of the dusty red sleigh and pulled myself in with my elbow. The sleigh-mobile was talking off, and I was halfway in with my legs dangling out the back. I stretched out, my fingertips grazing the violin. Jay was swerving around, trying to throw me off. This was what I always imagined it would be like to sneak a ride in Santa's sleigh—except Santa wouldn't be trying to kill me.

Jay slammed on the breaks. It flung me forward into the sleigh, but the breath was knocked clean out of me. It gave Jay time to grab the fiddle and hop out of the sleigh. I regained my breath and jumped after him—pushing him into the snow with the full weight of my landing. The sleigh-mobile was still running. He must be panicking to make a mistake like that. I wrenched the fiddle from his hands and turned to jump back into the sleigh. His arms swung around my ankles, and I face-planted into the snow. I yanked my left foot free and began throwing and kicking snow into his face. Both of us were yelling wildly—Jay's face covered in melty snow. I kicked my other leg free. I bolted into the front seat and pushed the gas pedal to the floor. Now I was doing donuts in the snow—being from the South didn't give me many experiences with snow driving.

Jay was standing up now with his hands out toward me like he was trying to calm a bucking bronco. I got straightened out, and a spray of snow whirled out behind me as I floored the gas pedal again, this time pointed in the right direction—the tower in my sights. Jay ran after me through the thick snow, but he quickly fell behind. I reached the tree, hopped out, and ran straight for the thick vines, which I hoped would lead to a doorway. Jay was shouting something unintelligible. He was getting closer, and he didn't want me to go in.

A dark opening yawned behind the vines. I shielded the fiddle by my side and stepped inside. I had to find somewhere to hide. I took another step. I needed to drop this fiddle off, go home, collect the rest of the money, and maybe even take in a few sights on the way. The crunch of snow signaled Jay's presence. *It's so dark.* I shuffled forward, barely taking steps at all—expecting to run into the wall at any moment. Darkness has a way of making spaces seem bigger than they are. It was like I was in a tunnel or a hallway rather than a slender tower.

"Melinda?"

I tried to quiet my shuffling steps, but I did not stop walking.

Jay's voice was shaky. "You do not know what you are getting yourself into here, my girl. You are well beyond your depths."

I tried not even to breathe. Why is everything so much louder in the dark?

Jay continued, "Horrifying creatures would give anything to have that instrument in their possession." He was gaining ground, and I tried to walk faster.

"I hear you," Jay said. Every time he spoke, it was closer. "You cannot do this on your own. Come back. We will make a plan."

The ground beneath my feet seemed to disappear. My feet continued to move mechanically forward. *My hands.* My knuckles were burning; my fingertips tingled. *Frostbite?* I did not loosen my hold on the violin.

Then, all at once, like someone flipping a switch, light came pouring in through an opening ahead. I trundled forward across the stone floor. I heeded Odessa's warning and stayed out of the light's path, and shielded my eyes from its rays. My back was flat against the stone wall of the tower.

"Come quick." Jay stayed back, but he was beckoning me to him. "Listen to me!" His voice was raspy and low. "Why do you think I live in the middle of the woods? I have to guard this entrance. It is not safe!"

What was ahead of me made me question my sanity; "Is that a . . . rainbow?" The wall of the cave-like surface had a huge split. Through this divide, flowing down like a waterfall was what appeared to be a rainbow. However, it was not exactly a rainbow. Each of the color bands raced forward. The colors were more vibrant than any rainbow I had ever seen. I might have been convinced I was dreaming if it were not for the pain. Even to look at the rainbow hurt my eyes. It was like the first blinding moment of a flashlight shining to the eyes, except this was a much deeper pain. Everything in me wanted to get away from it, but I refused to surrender to that creepy little man. I crept along the wall, still being careful to avoid stepping into the shaft of light. Unlike a waterfall, the rainbow belt made no sound. Strong wind hit my face. I squinted over the edge but couldn't make out any defining features.

"Gotcha!" Jay grabbed my wrist. He was now reaching for the fiddle in my other hand. I pulled away and stomped on his toes. He did not struggle or dodge my efforts. He attempted to pull me back down the hallway, but I continued to pull full force against him.

"Let go!"

He did not speak; his efforts fixed on the violin.

This guy is nuts. The only options were to turn back and give the prize to this madman or to go forward. *Forward it is.* I braced myself, turned the corner, and stepped out onto the rainbow, and as soon as I did, I was in blistering pain. I scrambled to get back to the dark entrance. Jay apparently didn't expect me to take the plunge and he, still grasping at the fiddle, fell over the ledge after me, but as soon as he fell, he released his grasp—flailing uncontrollably.

The fiddle was suddenly of no importance to him. I clawed at the entrance—Jay clamored to get over me—but the colorful bands swept us away without mercy. The rainbow, which appeared to be only light at first, became solid. First, the colors liquified and then became like gems. The weirdness of this didn't matter now. All that occupied my mind was the intense pain. It started from the inside out. It made all other hurts feel like skinned knees. I covered my ears as a loud screeching filled the air. It drifted to me as if from far away, but it was my screams.

The miserable brilliance of the colors shown right through my skin. I was turning into light myself—worse—I was fading away into nothing. Round and round the rainbow, we flew. The violin case vanished. My thin hand still grasped at the neck of the violin—which was as solid as ever. I would soon lose my hold on it.

Then the pain lessened abruptly. I was being lifted and dragged away from the excruciating colors. My hand was still thin but no longer transparent. Slowly, my eyes adjusted. I was under some sort of ledge. It cast a shadow over me. "I almost missed you! One more time around, and there would have been nothing left to save!"

I turned wide-eyed to look at the speaker. He, I suppose it was a he, was ashen. He must have been in this place longer than I because he was thin as paper. He must have been eight feet tall. Yet, even as thin as he was, he was not transparent, as I had been.

"You come from Soli?"

"I, I mean," I stammered, still disoriented, "I've come from Switzerland."

The strange creature shook his head. He was so huge. Even as he sat crouching, he towered over me. Over his shoulders was slung a black cloak. "Yes, you are from Soli. Now you are in Chaira. You must have got here by accident." He reached behind him and pulled out a cloak identical to the one across his shoulder. "You will need this here. It will keep you safe from the light."

I sat up slowly, still in shock, and accepted the cloak. "The light? Is that what is doing this?" I wrapped the cloak around me, and immediate relief washed over me. It was like aloe to a burn.

"The light is deadly," He scowled and glanced warily at the rainbow. "It is not safe to explain here." He pulled a dark hood over his sharp features. "Follow me."

Another scream rang through the air. *Jay.* "Wait."

The strange creature stopped.

"He's still on that rainbow belt of death!" I raised my eyebrows expectantly. He stared back at me. "What are you doing? We have to save him!"

"Isn't he your enemy?"

"Well, enemy might be a strong term, but we still can't let him disappear, or whatever."

The creature didn't move.

Seeing its hesitation, I pulled the cloak closer, preparing to dive after Swartzentruber myself. Something tugged at my cape. The strange creature gestured to another creature stumbling around. It was not as tall, but it was the same gray color—but something about it reminded me of— "Mr. Swartzentruber?" Although it changed him, it was undoubtedly him. Jay's voice spat curses into the calm. His lean figure and saunter were unchanged except in his color.

"Wait here," the creature said. "He will not last long like that."

I didn't argue and hurried back into the shade. The creature snuck over to Jay and offered him a cloak. To my surprise, Jay wasn't surprised by the creature as if he recognized him, although he didn't appear happy to see the strange creature. Jay snatched the cloak which the creature offered and rushed over to the shade of another boulder. The creature followed him calmly.

They were out of my sight now. Giant boulders—some bigger than the trees—littered the surrounding landscape. I rubbed my eyes. I've always been one to go with the flow, but this is crazy. It had to be some sort of bizarre dream, but this pain was worse than a pinch. I glanced down at my skin, half expecting it to be gray like the others, but it was unchanged. "Come!" The shadow-like creature appeared again, "We must leave at once."

"But what about—"

"Poor fool has chosen another way. We must keep clear of him."

I didn't argue and timidly followed my strange rescuer.

CHAPTER 11

"THIS WAY!" THE SHADOW CREATURE's long hands urged me toward a small hole in the ground that the bushes had hidden. "Underground is the only place to hide from the burning. It is safe there or nearly safe. We are never completely free of it. The light weasels its way into every crevice, but underground mostly blots it out."

It took a moment to wiggle through, but inside was a roomy underground chamber. The creature covered up the entryway with some dry branches, and the burning sensations lessened, but it was not pitch black even in the cave, and a dull ache still radiated through my bones.

"Please make yourself comfortable," the shadow creature said, motioning to a pile of moss-like substance.

"I'm sorry to intrude."

"Oh no intrusion, young Soli, none! It is a delight to have a guest. These are dangerous times, you know, and one doesn't host much company."

I plopped down on the moss couch. "I have never seen anything like this place."

"Yes, yes. I have met people from Soli before. Your land is a wonderful place if the stories are true."

"Soli?"

"It is what we here call the land from which you came. I must say, you are handling it a lot better than the others who have found our lands. Most of them spend the first several hours doing all manner of ridiculous stunts—trying to wake themselves up or escape in some other bizarre fashion. You, overall, are calm."

"Yeah, well, I've read enough to know that would be a waste of time." I dragged my hand over the barren walls of this underground oasis. "But I would like to know what the danger is exactly, and what is with the light?" *Odessa never said anything about other worlds with crazy sunburn.*

The creature let out a mournful sigh. "I'm afraid the answer to both questions is one and the same. A great tyrant rules our land. He causes the light to burn and terrorize all who dwell in his reach."

"A tyrant? With the power to curse the light?" I asked skeptically. *Please let me be in some weird airplane sleep.*

"Yes, he is powerful and full of jealousy." The creature paced back and forth. "He wishes to be feared, yet he is afraid that one day there will rise one who will overpower him. So, he created a burning light to make all his subjects frail, so no one would ever rise against him."

"How many 'subjects' are there?"

"Oh, many live in his kingdom," the shadow creature lowered his voice, "but not all are subject to him." He leaned in closer. "Some of us—" the shadow creature glanced behind him, "—some of us live in secret, hiding from the burning, and one day we hope to be strong enough to start an uprising and overthrow the tyrant."

I rubbed my chin. "Okay. Well, good luck with that. Sounds like a great cause. I have a cause of my own I need to deal with. I need to return this, and then I'll be on my way." I lifted the violin out from under my cloak. A brilliant light exuded from it, and I nearly dropped it.

"Put it back! Put it back!" The creature shrieked, "Do not wait! I'm fading!"

I quickly stuffed it back under the dark cloak. It brushed against my side and seared my skin.

"Where did you get that?" the creature fumed.

"I was given it." I stammered, "I'm supposed to bring it back here, I guess."

This news calmed the creature.

"I am instructed to return it to its place," I quickly pulled out the note, "behind the waterfall."

"Oh no, no, no," the creature said, "that would be the worst place of all."

"Why?"

"Well," it drew closer, "that is exactly where it belongs, you see."

I stared at him blankly. *Odessa better pay me double for this.*

"We are attempting to rebel against the strongholds of his kingdom, and this thing," he said with disgust, "is part of his kingdom."

"Well, I feel for you, I really do, but I'm getting paid to take it behind the waterfall. Doing my job, ya know?"

"We must destroy it, and we must destroy it as soon as possible. This is our in."

I pulled at my face in exasperation. "Okay, you know what? I don't care. You can have the stupid fiddle. Use it for kindling for all I care. I need to go home. I didn't agree to all this," I threw my hands up, gesturing to the dark den around me, "and I'd be happy to sell you the fiddle."

The creature was silent for a moment. "Well, young Soli, how do you plan to get back to your home?"

"I'll-I mean, I can . . . " I swallowed slowly.

"I know the way back to your country."

"Well, I know the way back too! Up that cliff and through the cave."

"Right, that is what you might consider an entrance only. It is impossible to get back up the cliff alive, but I know another way."

"Great! I'll follow you then."

"Yes, and I'll gladly take you there . . . if you will help destroy the instrument. That is my price for your return home."

I stared at the shadow creature. He had the upper hand. "What is with you people and this fiddle, and why is it that everyone wants me to do the dirty work?"

"We need a Soli—you can withstand the light longer than us Chairians." The shadow creature tilted its head. "What do you say?"

"Let me get this straight—I help you destroy this instrument, and you will get me home?"

"That would be the deal."

"Fine," I sighed. "What do you want me to do?" *Odessa would never know the difference anyway.*

The creature tapped its fingers with excitement, "We need to make a plan to demolish it. Yes, this may be what we need."

It was like holding hot coals under my cloak. I was afraid the instrument would soon burn right through me. "Let's do it now. Can we burn it?"

"No, any form of light belongs to the enemy. "

"Smash it?

"Yes," the creature said thoughtfully, "Yes, that might work. But there is only one place to do it."

I attempted to wrap the instrument in the cloak to keep it away from my skin, but the heat went straight through the fabric. "Where?"

"The canyon. It is the only place with rocks solid enough to destroy the instrument, and it is the farthest from the tyrant's reach. Only there can everything be made right. "

I shifted my weight again. The burning was becoming unbearable now. "Right. So how long is this going to take?"

"We will have to travel carefully to avoid being seen. If one of the enemy spies were to capture us, we would undoubtedly be destroyed."

"Destroyed?" I stammered.

"The enemy will entice you to join his ranks, but if you refused, he would undoubtedly blot you out on the spot."

It takes a lot to shake me, but the threat of being blotted out on the spot gets me every time. "No offense, but if the choice is to join the tyrant or 'be destroyed,' I'm joining the tyrant."

"Young Soli, you do not understand?"

"I understand that I've changed my mind, and you can take the violin yourself. I want to go home."

"No!" The creature gained height and strength. "No, I cannot take it. Only you can destroy the instrument."

"Why does everyone keep saying that?" I wanted to scream. "You're too afraid to go, so you send me?"

"I consider it an honor to go on this quest, but my arms cannot carry any object made of light. You are from Soli and are made differently. I have lived in Chaira for too long. I would not have the strength to destroy this blasted instrument." The creature lowered his voice, "I need you, you see. My people need you." He hesitated, "This is what we need to free us from the tyrant's reign."

I sighed. "Great for you, but how're you going to keep your end of the bargain if I'm 'blotted out'?"

"I have already saved your life once. Trust me, I won't leave your side."

I let out a slow breath as I weighed my options and concluded, once again, that I didn't have any. If I wanted any chance of getting home to see my family or a penny of that reward money, I was going to have to take the shadow creature up on his offer. He was right; he had saved my life once before, and I had no other option but to trust him. I rolled my eyes. "Fine. When do we leave? Should we travel by night?"

"Ah, night. We have fairytales of such a marvelous time in far-off lands. Here there is no night—only blistering day." The creature sighed. "Rest first. It may be the last chance we get for some time."

CHAPTER 12

S TEPPING OUT OF THE PRIMITIVE berm was like sticking my
face into an oven. My first instinct was to cover my eyes,
but this did nothing as the burning pierced right through my
skin. I pulled my cloak tighter around me. "Y'all need to invent
sunscreen."

The shadow creature pulled me into the shade of a boulder.
We darted from shadow to shadow. "We must always be on the
lookout for the tyrant's soldiers."

"How will I know if I see one?"

"You will know. Shining ones are like the tyrant himself and
burn all in their path."

My eyes flitted around the landscape. It was the first time I
had a chance to take in this peculiar world. Everything had a scaly
appearance—not like a reptile scaly but more like shingles on a
roof. Everything had layers—organized layers. Unlike our world,
nothing here was random. It was as if every rock and every speck
of dirt had been placed in its spot. It reminded me of my grand-
mother's house. She had shelves of unimportant knick-knacks, yet
she used her specific system to arrange each one. Even the leaves
on the trees were meticulously ordered.

It was as if I was walking around in a painting. The trees and
plants had the appearance of a strong wind constantly blowing, yet
the air was still. The scattering of enormous boulders all around
was as if giants were having a game of marbles.

The sky was a pinkish-orange color, but there was no sun or source of light anywhere. The shadow creature moved swiftly from shade to shade—constantly glancing around, looking for danger. It appeared to be second nature to be on the lookout for the tyrant. I tried to keep a sharp eye out too, but the cumbersome hood cut off my field of vision.

A flash that reminded me of lightning lit up the sky. A sharp pain struck me. It hurt the most around the side I carried the violin, but the ache moved through all my limbs. It was like a full-body migraine and wasp sting at the same time. I jumped behind the nearest boulder. The shadow creature must have also dashed to a different shelter. I wrapped the dark cloak around myself tightly but pushed the hood off my forehead, looking in all directions frantically—no one—I then pulled the hood down over my eyes once again. I sniffed. The air smelled of singed hair. My hand flew up under my hood. My hair was hot to the touch even after just a brief second out from under the hood. *No, no time to check.*

I peeked out of my hiding place. The surroundings were as peaceful as ever. No sign of any tyrant soldiers and no sign of the shadow creature. I was afraid to stay in one spot for too long, so I quietly stepped out and hurried to the next shade—looking in all directions for the shadow creature. *Staring at the sun for ten seconds can blind you. If I stay here much longer, this place will gouge my eyes out.* I trudged on. The creature did not reappear.

He needs me as much as I need him. I repeated to myself as I attempted to slow my breathing. I slipped a hand over the protruding lump under my cloak. The scalding heat drove back my hand. *Definitely still there. I need a backup plan.* There must be some other way to escape all this. *Odessa's note.* I shook my head. Maybe Jay told the truth when he said things have changed since they were here last. Even Odessa had inferred that the violin was possessed or something. And who knows how long it had been since Odessa had even been in this place. The tyrant might not even have been in control yet. I stumbled into a boulder wall. What if Odessa had sent me on this job with no intention of me ever finding my way home? I inhaled sharply. I had to figure this out on my own.

I pushed the hood back off my head again. The immediate pain was insufferable, but I had to look around. "No sign of any waterfalls," I muttered. In the distance, a jagged scar was drawn across the face of this perfect world. It was the only spot I surveyed without my eyes getting fried over easy. It had to be the canyon the shadow creature was talking about. In a split second, I had my plan of action. I slung my hood back on. If I kept my eyes on the canyon, I could make it there, and hopefully, the shadow creature would reappear on the way. Yes. He was my best shot at getting out here. I began once again, running from shadow to shadow, with the violin thumping at my side.

CHAPTER 13

I SCRAMBLED OVER A ROCKY LEDGE. The bleak refuge of the canyon was no closer than when I had begun. The beauty of Chaira—more dazzling than anything I had ever seen in my world—mocked my every step. It was heaven and hell as one. No, it was hell—the beauty of heaven all around, but no means to enjoy it. It was a starving man with a warm, steamy meal placed out of reach or like this fiddle—a beautiful instrument but no way to be played.

Light glinted from behind the bushes. I froze. The leaves rustled, and the light grew more intense. "Maybe it is a cute little animal, like a deer or a kitten?" I hoped aloud. Then, remembering the painful rainbows in this world, I didn't stick around to meet a unicorn. I slung the bagged violin over my shoulder and ran straight into the open light. Whatever it was, it must have seen me because as soon as I ran, light lashed out from behind me. The violin hit my shoulder hard, but I kept running. Its steps were lighter than mine, and it quickly gained on me. The blinding light stung my eyes and tore at my skin. I lunged behind the boulder—pressing myself between the earth and rock.

Silence. I cautiously opened my eyes, half expecting to see a beast bearing down on me. Nothing. It had to be here somewhere. I listened intently, then slowly peered around the crevice.

It shone brightly and was as beautiful and terrible as everything else in Chaira. I pulled back into the safety of the shadow.

It had seen me and appeared to be beckoning me. Its long silvery arms fluttered in the air like moonbeams. Its voice was music: "Come! Come here! Don't be afraid. I have a message for you." Its beauty grated on me, and even though its voice should have been lovely, it was like nails on a chalkboard to my ears.

"Don't move." A hand covered my mouth. I turned, and to my surprise, the shadow creature sat beside me. I pushed his hand down. "Where did you go?"

"No time for questions. This way."

I scrambled after him, and he led us away from shining one and into a wooded path. The roots reached for my ankles, and tree branches lashed out like whips as if to bar my way, but I pressed on. I would not lose him this time. The violin scorched my hand, but I did not loosen my grip. "Where are we going?" My voice was only a raspy whisper.

"Somewhere safe," the shadow replied. "Somewhere the light does not reach."

CHAPTER 14

ALTHOUGH THE SHINING ONE WAS not pursuing us, I still had the feeling it would pounce at any moment. We turned the corner, and a river appeared before us. I was so focused on running that I didn't even hear its roar.

"You can swim?" The shadow creature leered at the bright reflections bouncing off the intense rapids.

"Yes, of course." I repositioned the fiddle and longed for the cold water.

The creature pulled a black rope out of his cloak. "Tie this around your waist, and never stop swimming."

The rope was cool and comforting. As I tied it around me, the sting went out of my fingers.

"The tyrant's soldiers guard the river. It leads to his throne. We must hasten."

"What if we get caught?"

"Not an option." And with this, the shadow creature ran out into the open toward the river's sandy bank. The rope yanked me after him, and my hood fell back from my head. The sand sent fragments of light piercing my face like needles. Headbutting a porcupine would have been less painful. Then came the river. It was fresh lava on my feet. I shrieked and pulled against the pain, but the rope towed me deeper into the molten stream.

"Stop!" The shining one clasped my arm. Its touch left a deep burn. I yelled, and it released me. The water that had promised to be so refreshing hit my face with the force of a blacksmith's mallet. I was now fully submerged. As we swam deeper and deeper, my only comfort was the rope, and even it was getting thinner. I no longer held the satchel with the precious violin. My energy was focused on the burning and struggling against it. However, as the creature hauled me further into the water, the pain lessened. The darkness grew, and it was like a salve on my scorched skin. Soon the light disappeared completely, and for the first time since I had been in this strange land, I felt almost no pain.

Even the instrument strung around my waist had lost much of its heat.

I had been holding my breath this whole time, and now my lungs burned with the urgent need for fresh air—any air. I grasped the taut rope and began to pull myself forward, hand over hand, closing the distance between me and the creature. Then, without warning, we burst out of the water, and something firm was in front of me. The creature dragged me onto the dry ground. The burning had disappeared almost entirely, but it was like when you've been in the sun all day and get a bad sunburn. Even when you are indoors, your skin still retains some of the heat.

It was can't-see-my-hand-in-front-of-my-face dark. "Where are we?"

"These are the ancient caverns. Carved out by water ages ago. We found them at the beginning of the rebellion." The creature's voice was low, and his words drawn out. "We await the day when we can overthrow the tyrant. This way. To the Shadow Village. You will be safe there until we make our plans."

CHAPTER 15

T HE AIR WAS CRISP, ALMOST cold, and it soothed my aching muscles, and the darkness calmed my tired eyes. The rope gently pulled me along, and soon, the city came alive. I had never toured a city without my sight. Even the blackest of nights always had streetlights, car headlights, and the flicker of houses and stores all around. The moon and stars shone as nightlights in the country, but it was nothing but pitch black and noise here. Something touched my shoulder, and a deep, "Pardon me," rushed past. All of this did not leave me uneasy; on the contrary, I breathed a sigh of relief for the first time since entering this country.

A delicious smell wafted through the air. It reminded me of pizza. I hadn't eaten anything since I had come to this world, and my growling stomach questioned how long it would be until the next meal. We must have been in the town's heart now because the passersby bustle was all around me. I'm sure my knuckles were white with my determination not to let go of the rope that connected me to the shadow creature. The fiddle still rested securely in the satchel. It miraculously stayed with me through the swim, and now it was my only source of discomfort in this shadow haven. Even with no light here, the fiddle still had some heat. It was not enough to provide any genuine pain, and I was reasonably successful in ignoring it; even so, it was like having a thorn lodged in my back—easy to forget until I reclined.

However, food was still at the forefront of my mind. The appetizing smell was growing stronger. *I hope we are almost there. How does everyone navigate around here? That's odd.* My arm brushed against something metallic. Visions of a knight in a suit of armor flashed through my mind. However, the object was stationary. And then my elbow scraped another metal something. The surrounding crowd grew thinner, and our steps were on an incline. I cautiously let one hand fall from the rope and stretched out to see what I might find.

I immediately came in contact with the metal. It was a smooth sheet. I slid my fingers along it as we walked. Up and down—it was tall and wide. Then it was gone. My hand drifted in mid-air for a moment until I came brusquely up against another metal sheet. *A wall. Houses?* The delicious smell was now torturous. A moment more, and my stomach would eat itself.

The rope pulled me to the left. We had been walking uphill till now. I kept my hand out, but it knocked hard against what I assumed to be a door frame. It was a very narrow opening, only big enough for me to slide through. The pleasant smell was in here.

"Melinda, I would like you to meet your host family. You will stay here with them until our plans are complete."

Bodies rustled. "You're not leaving again, are you?" I asked, not hiding my concern.

"You will be perfectly safe here. I trust Diume with my life."

"As I trust you with mine, Daveechi."

Daveechi? I guess that is the shadow creature's name. It had never crossed my mind to wonder if he had a name.

Heavy footsteps came forward. "We will see that you are protected and provided for," a gruff voice said. I assumed this to be Diume.

"This is Oi-u and Onn."

"Hello," two voices chorused.

"You must be hungry," a lighter voice to my right said, "Onn go make a plate for our guest."

CHAPTER 16

THE SHADOW CREATURE WAS TALKING in hushed tones to Diume and the one I assumed to be Diume's wife. They must be discussing me, but I didn't care. My focus was on the food in front of me. As soon as the plate clattered onto the table, I reached for it, not bothering to wait to see if they would offer me utensils, and my hand touched something soft with crisp flecks scattered on top. It was not hot, although it was not cold either. It was good enough to satisfy any Goldilocks out there. I bit into the thick chunk, and to this day, I cannot tell you what it was. Only that it had a weird texture and was the kind of food that, under any other circumstances, I would have skipped over in a buffet line, but today I would have eaten rocks if they were adequately salted.

I had soon finished it. *Still hungry.* I searched blindly around the table in front of me. Surely there must be more than that. *This wouldn't satisfy a kitten.*

"They ration it out. There will be more tomorrow." The voice was like Diume's—solemn and straightforward—, but it was lighter and gentle, like Oi-u.

I was startled and then embarrassed to be caught searching for more food. *He must be the son. Onn, was it?* "How do you get food here?" I asked aloud, half to myself and half to the chance Onn was still seated across from me.

"We raid the tyrant's storehouses."

"Is that dangerous?"

"The tyrant has no end of food. He does not need to set up a watch and does not even realize that we took anything."

I frowned. "If the tyrant does not notice, why not take more?"

"The food is infused with light and must go through a month-long process before it is edible. Much of the food we bring does not make it through the process, and it is difficult to carry large amounts because of the light."

"How could you let this happen!" An angry voice broke from the hushed conversation, then sunk back into words not loud enough to understand but loud enough to hear the urgency that quickly followed.

I sat quietly—trying to catch any stray words. Onn did not speak again. The discussion in the corner returned to a lighter tone, and shuffling steps approached. A thin hand lighted on my shoulder.

"Melinda, I must go. You are in excellent hands until I return." The hand dropped. "I'll come to get you once we have secured a safe path. Take care of your cargo. Keep it with you at all times." And with that, the shadow creature—Daveechi—swept through the door frame, and I was alone with strangers I couldn't see.

Oi-u broke the silence. "Allow me to show you to your resting place." Her voice was kind and soft. The rope was no longer around my waist. Of course, the shadow creature must have taken it with him. I started a few halted steps forward. My heart pounded as I forced images of a snake-covered floor from my mind. My arms extended in front of me as I tried to walk as normally as possible, but I moved forward at an uneasy halting pace. *Did these people have night vision? How do they live like this?*

A gentle hand grasped my arm. "Whhhaaaaooooww," I cried out, first from being startled and second from the immediate pain it inflicted. Childhood nightmares of being attacked by an unknown boogie man lurking in the dark were becoming all too real.

"You are hurt!" Oi-u's melodic voice had a calming effect. "Sit back down, and I will bandage your burn."

I tentatively reached behind me for the table and eased myself back down. "How did you know it was a burn?" I asked, leaning the injured arm on the table.

"Our people come home from foraging with wounds far worse than this." She said gently, "You must be strong to have made it through the Tyrant's lands with only this minor injury."

The suave was refreshing. It reminded me of my own mom and the countless times she took care of the scrapes and bruises I accrued growing up. I held back a sigh. *This is all Aidan Odessa's fault. No money was worth this, and she had to be well aware of that.* I scowled in the darkness. *But if I make it out of this alive, I better get paid double—no triple!*

"There." Oi-u's voice brought me back to the current strange reality.

"That feels so much better," I said with surprise.

Oi-u took my hand. "This way. You will need some rest after your journey." I followed quietly like a child being put to bed. "Thank you, Mrs. Oi-u."

"Get some rest now, Soli."

I eased myself into the bed I was given. *Ah! Bed. Sleep.* It was even better than food. The creatures' home must be a one-room house. I was not taken through any more doorways but was led to a corner of the room. Oi-u's footsteps pattered around, and dishes clanked. The darkness provided all the privacy I needed. The resting place was a giant floor pillow. It was round with curved pillowed walls and soft all around—like a massive dog bed. It was comfortable. I curled up, trying to push away fears and memories of home, and waited for sleep to come.

CHAPTER 16

O NN WOKE ME UP AT what I presume to be an ungodly hour. But who's to say? I now sympathize with the Alaskans.

"You will go with me today," Onn said. I had no idea he was standing over me, and I instinctively clutched the cloaked violin. I half expected it to be gone, or maybe I only hoped it would be, but it hung by my side—my own personal ball and chain.

"Where are we going?" I asked, trying to sound as if he had not made me jump out of my skin.

"Come," his voice was now a few feet in front of me, "I will take you around our village."

I pushed myself up from the pillowy bed and cautiously walked forward toward Onn's voice. The first thing I ran into was the table, and then, almost immediately after recovering from my stumble, I walked into a wall. Onn came to my rescue. He took hold of my wrist gently in a way that reminded me of his mother and led me forward.

"Here, do you feel that?" His voice was patient. "On the floor?"

"I don't feel anything."

"Are your feet covered?"

"I am wearing shoes, if that is what you mean," I said, trying not to sound sarcastic.

"Take them off."

"Ok . . . " I removed what was left of my boots, now feeling even more exposed to whatever monsters might lurk in the dark.

"There." He led me forward a little further. He was still holding my wrist. "Do you feel it now? The bumps in the floor?"

"Yes, I do!" It felt like embedded quarters along the floor to make a little path. It was like braille for my feet.

"If you walk along the path, you will be fine." He paused as if thinking, "But since you are new at this, you best hold on to me for now." He slipped his hand down into mine.

I yanked my hand free. "I can do it."

"Suit yourself, Lindy," and I could have sworn I heard him smile.

"It's Melinda," I said in a huff. "Where are we going today, anyway?" I asked as I shuffled my feet across the studded path. My toes wished for sunny barefoot creek hikes.

"I am going to show you around today. Perhaps take you to the food mill later. That is where I work." He paused. "Are your feet okay? Those of us here are used to it and have calloused feet. The path might hurt soft feet."

"Who you calling soft-feet?" I said, "I run barefoot over gravel all the time—doesn't faze me."

"Ok, well, stay close."

I patted around the narrow doorway in front of me and slid through it quickly this time. The quartered road split in front of me, and Onn placed his hand on my shoulder and turned me to the right. The path sloped downward. My hand slid across the cold metal walls once more. I walked one foot in front of the other in the studded path and curled my toes around the circular bumps.

The bustle of the Shadow Village began once again. I was being jostled and shoved from all sides. People were shouting and moving faster to get around me. I struggled to maintain my balance, but my feet were no longer on the jutted path. Now I was pressed up against a metal home. Everything happened in about a minute, although it felt like an eternity; however, before I panicked, a hand slipped into mine. Already, I recognized it as the same hand that had held mine earlier, and Onn's voice was beside me, "Perhaps you will allow me to guide you now, Lindy?" The teasing tone was in his voice once again. Sarcasm is as alive and thriving in this world as it is in my own. I was miffed, but I didn't let go of his hand. It was not much of a tour to go through the dark village, but even if everything were visible, I imagined there still wouldn't be a lot to see.

"We build all our homes the same," Onn explained as we tunneled through like a couple of ants in an underground maze. "It is a grid. We build each house with the same dimensions and distance apart from each other. Each road has four houses on each square—two on each side."

"If everything's the same, how do you find your way?"

"Here, I will show you." Onn pulled me quickly to the left. We walked a few paces forward before a sing-song chorus of children's voices reached us. "This is the school," he said. "This section of town is built differently from the houses. The school takes up a complete square, and beyond the school are the factories. We will go there next." He began walking again. "Every shadling must go to school to learn—" He paused as if wondering how much to explain, "well, we learn many things: how to measure using a ramping log, the exact size and dimensions of each square, how the food processor works and of the dangers of the overworld, how to understand hydraulic time, and how to read each square map." He stopped and pulled my hand over a rough surface on the metal wall. My fingers recognized lines and shapes, and I concluded this must be a square map, but I didn't know what any of it meant. Onn did not stop, however, but simply kept walking and explaining. "We learn the complete history of both Chairi and Soli."

"Chairi is your world, and Soli is mine."

"Right," Onn said, his voice upbeat, "but one of the first things we memorize is the village grid. Every villager has a map in their mind. We know every turn, every corner, and every plot by memory."

"Don't you ever get lost?"

"Maybe when we were young, but how would it look if we got lost now when we learn to memorize the grid since year one?"

Like forgetting the ABCs.

"They teach us how to fight in battle. Everyone trains for war to prepare for the day when we will overthrow the tyrant." Onn began walking again, his hand still clasped mine, and pulled me forward.

"How long do you go to school?" I asked.

"Only until year fifty."

"Fifty?" I gasped. "How old are you?"

"I am only seventy. Which is why I am stuck leading you around."

"Seventy? I am only nineteen."

Onn stopped, and with that same smile in his voice, said, "Calm down, Soli. We measure time differently here. Like I was saying earlier, the hydraulic clocks help us keep time."

"Is that some sort of water clock?" I asked.

"Yes, exactly. The one thing we have in abundance down here is water," Onn sighed. With that, he walked on, dragging me behind, wondering what kind of time measurement they used and whether this was an old man leading me or if his voice was as young as it sounded.

"Here. We are coming to the factory squares."

Machinery hummed, and workers bustled around me. In my mind's eye, I pictured tiny cartoon ants all running around in tan uniforms. One ant is holding a clipboard and ordering the worker ants around. Each ant has an assignment, and they march down the dirt tunnels carrying piles of food on their heads and not stopping for nothing or nobody.

Onn startled me out of my daydreaming, "This is the food refining factory where I work. There is also the clothing mill, the metal refinery, and the pathmaker squares."

"What about the team that goes to get the supplies, you know, from up there?" I had to shout to be understood over all the factory noise.

"It is dangerous work. Daveechi chooses who will be on the teams himself. There are casualties."

"So, what is your job?"

"Come, I'll show you." He pulled me toward the left edge of the square. "Here." He put my fingers on some sliding wooden beads that I guessed were part of an abacus counter. "I keep track of the food packaged and make sure the correct amount gets rationed out per household. It takes—"

"You're the one with the clipboard!" I started.

"The what?"

"Umm, you are the one in charge," I laughed nervously.

"I guess you could say—"

"Onn! Who's that with you?"

Instead of introducing me, Onn edged me behind him. "A visitor."

More footsteps.

"Visitor? We don't get visitors here. Where is your visitor from?"

"Soli." Onn jerked my hand before I had the chance to say more.

"Soli?" a new speaker said.

"Does Daveechi know?" The first voice interrupted.

"Of course he does, Avis," Onn retorted. "She's an asset to us."

"Hear that, Deem?" Avis laughed. "A Soli is an asset."

"Yeah, too bad it was her kind who got us here, to begin with," Deem said.

"You two need to back off," a higher-pitched voice said.

"Whatever. We came to see if you were going to join us tonight." Avis took a step closer.

Onn's grip tightened around my hand. "Are you crazy? Lower your voice."

"Will you relax? No one knows what I'm talking about."

"Silence, Avis!" the higher voice ordered. "Your carelessness will land us all in the hut."

Onn sighed, "Lindy, these are my benighted friends."

One of the new voices laughed boisterously. "He is one of us, whatever he says."

Feet plodded a couple of steps toward me. "I'm Deem. The loudmouth is Avis, and the angry one is Magoumi."

I smiled and nodded and then, realizing no one could see me doing this, said, "Um, nice to meet you."

"This is Lindy," Onn said.

"Well, actually, it's Melin—"

"Liiiindyyy!" said Deem, "So you're bringing her tonight, yeah, Onn?"

"What makes you think that would be a good idea?" Magoumi must have shoved him because feet shuffled in a struggle to maintain balance.

"Hey, Daveechi brought her here. She may have more information. Onn said she was an asset," Deem said.

"Will you all keep it down! You know he has ears everywhere," Onn said through his teeth, "Now, get out of here, and I'll see you tonight."

"Whatever you say, Onn." Deem shuffled away.

"Out. See you tonight." Avis's footsteps were more of a trot.

Magoumi stayed rooted in her spot. "Hey Onn, as much as I hate to admit it, I agree with Deem for once. Bring the girl tonight."

Onn grunted some semblance of a reply as she walked away.

I was silent until the footsteps faded. "What was that about?"

"Listen, please don't tell anyone about this conversation—especially not Oi-u and Diume."

I smirked, "Son, you've got nothing to worry about. I'm the master of sneaking around. Of course, sneaking around is kinda what got me in the whole mess to begin with."

"Will you please keep it down!"

"Oh, right." I said, lowering my voice to a whisper, "You don't want nobody to know, well, ain't nobody going to hear it from me."

CHAPTER 18

For the rest of the day, Onn spoke of nothing except the different aspects of the town. A shrill whistle blew, signaling a lunch break, and Onn handed me a portion of the same stuff I had eaten the night before.

"What is this anyway?"

"What do you mean? It is food," Onn replied shortly.

"No, I mean, what is this particular dish called?"

"Do you name all your dishes in Soli? What about the silverware? Do they get christened as well?"

"What are you talking about? I mean the recipe. What is this recipe?"

"This is the only food we have. It is not a recipe; it is food. While you are here, you will eat three portions a day, and it will always be the same. It is food. The only food."

"Can't you have some variety? Ya know, 'variety is the spice of life,' and all that?"

"Not in the Shadow Village."

I spent the rest of the day following Onn around at work. He was good at what he did. I felt childish holding his hand all day, but everyone was rushing about in a whole lot of ordered chaos that I was afraid to let go, especially after meeting Deem, Magoumi, and Avis. Not everyone in this village was as welcoming as Onn and Daveechi.

By the end of the day, I was so tired I practically slept walked back to Diume's home. By the time I had eaten the "food" here for the third time, I was already growing tired of it. *Imagine eating the same thing every day, three times a day for a lifetime.*

Oi-u bustled about the small home cleaning the dishes after dinner. She took my plate. "Thank you," I said softly.

Oi-u touched my shoulder. "How was your day, children?"

"It was good," I answered instinctively. Oi-u reminded me so much of my mother, making me even more homesick.

"Did Onn take you around all the squares?"

"I think so," I said, suppressing a yawn.

"Only the Westside and the factory squares," Onn said.

"Did you meet anyone?" Oui asked.

"We met—"

"Lindy—" Onn sputtered.

"Well, I mean, we met no one . . . really."

"Onn," Oi-u began, "I hope you—"

"Who did you meet?" Diume thundered from the far corner.

"Deem. We met Deem," Onn said.

"Onn, you know that boy is not someone to introduce Melinda to," Oi-u said softly.

"She is in your charge, and you are to do what is best for her!" Diume's voice was stern, but the anger was draining from his voice.

"We happened to run into him," I said, taking a cue from Onn, "We only spoke with him for a moment."

Onn was silent.

Diume grunted, "See that you keep it that way."

"It is late." Oi-u said, "Why don't we all go to rest."

A shuffle commenced as the remaining dishes were put away, and Oi-u helped me find my resting place. I listened as her steps pattered to the other side of the room. Diume and Oi-u were speaking softly.

"Onn?" I was not sure that he was anywhere close.

"Lindy."

Very close.

"It's Melinda. Listen," I lowered my voice, "I want to go."

"Go?"

"You know, go . . . " My voice was barely audible now, " . . . to the meeting with you tonight."

"Shhhh." Onn put his hand on mine. "Why does everyone have such big mouths today?"

"I want to go."

Onn sighed, "We must wait. Sleep now."

'Go to sleep, and I will wake you up when it's time.' I'm the oldest of six kids, mister. I know every trick in the book. I lay awake, waiting for footsteps.

CHAPTER 19

A N HOUR OR SO LATER, a stirring on the loose dirt floor alerted me that Onn was on the move. I sat up, listening intently. Now how to get up and follow without him noticing. He would, of course, naturally have sharper senses than me and probably would hear the first step I took. I sat perfectly still. Then there was a sound of cloth scraping against the doorframe and silence. I crept slowly across the room and poked my head out the doorway. The street was quiet except for the whisper of Onn's footsteps. I curled my toes on the bumpy trail and tried not to make a sound as I followed behind him. Once we got far enough away from the house, I would reveal that I was following him, but we would be too far away for him to send me back by that point.

Onn was moving more carefully, which was good because I wouldn't keep up if he had traveled as he did during the day. Not another soul was out. *What time is it? No one has any late-night parties around here, apparently.* I had to make sure I kept a steady pace. It was essential to move quickly enough not to lose him, but to maintain my distance, so he did not hear me following him. The empty streets made it easier to follow. It was not nearly as intimidating to be without sight when I wasn't traveling through a buffalo stampede.

I paused. Onn's patter had disappeared. *How did I lose him so quickly? No, he must have stopped.* I listened again: nothing. I groped along the metal walls looking for where he might have turned. A much harsher set of footsteps rushed from around the corner. I plastered myself against the metal home beside me. Behind the commanding footfalls came a softer pattering. I slid down the sleek wall and crouched on the ground—trying not to breathe. The angry footsteps spoke: "I have it under control," it hissed.

Daveechi.

"I've become accustomed to a certain standard of living," a deep voice said.

That voice. I recognized it immediately.

"Not here." Daveechi said, "They do not understand, nor will they if I can protect them from it."

"Yeah, yeah," the deep voice continued, seemingly unconcerned with stealth, "I can see how you are 'protecting them.' Don't try to pull one over on me. Keep your end of the deal, and I'll keep mine."

The two of them were walking toward me now.

"I don't see how you have much of this situation under control at all. The food rations are growing smaller each year, and the light is growing stronger—"

Daveechi stopped in the road. He was right in front of me. My breath threatened to tickle his ankles. "I said not here!" The rage in Daveechi's voice made me question if it was really him.

The other voice did not speak again, and they continued to walk. When the two footfalls faded, I listened carefully for Onn's step to reappear. *This can't be happening.* I pushed myself up from the ground and leaped back to the braille pathway. There was nothing but panic now, and I ran full force ahead—hands flailing in front of me. Forget secrecy; I was going to be lost forever in this darkness.

My toe caught on one of the bumps in the pathway, and I went sprawling forward. My arm scraped across the roadway. I did not have time to think about this, however, because my other hand landed against something boney and warm. *It's a foot!*

"Onn?" I whispered.

"Melinda?" The voice was familiar, but it was not Onn.

"Who's there?"

"Hush, now, you are going to wake the whole village. It's me, Magoumi."

Magoumi placed her hand on my elbow, and I slowly got up. "You don't know how happy I am to find you. How'd you know it was me?"

"Ha!" Magoumi scoffed and helped me up. "Come on, we're going to be late." Her hand dropped from my elbow, and her confident stride sauntered away. "Will you back off? I can feel you breathing on my neck."

"Oh, sorry." I slowed my pace and tried to control my faltering breath, but I stayed close. I wasn't going to risk being alone in this village again.

"This way." Magoumi grabbed my sleeve and pulled me around a corner, but then stopped, and I ran right into her. The satchel with the fiddle swung forward and hit her arm. "Ow!" She swung around. "What is that?"

"None of your business."

"Listen, you little glop, I didn't have to help you, and if you are going to play games with me, I can leave you right here. And trust me, we are so far out that no one will ever find you, and I don't have to be with you long to know that you can never find your way back. Now I'm going to ask you one more time, what touched me?"

"I will tell you this much: you felt the pain of a brush with it. Do you want me to unleash its full power?" I said, trying to sound as intimidating as she did, "Because I won't hesitate—"

"Lindy?"

"Onn!" I had never been so happy to not see someone in my entire life.

"What are you doing here?"

I squared my shoulders. "You left without me, so I followed you here."

"Pfff!" Magoumi jeered, "whatever, I had to rescue your little project here. She was tripping all over herself."

I was about to light into her, but Onn pulled me away, and I'd never figure out where she was unless she spoke again.

"Lindy, you shouldn't be here."

"Well," I said, still thinking about lunging in the general direction of where Magoumi might be, "I am here, and that's how it is."

"Will you all stop squawking and get in here." The voice came from below me.

"Be right there, Deem." Magoumi's voice disappeared from in front of me.

Onn grabbed my hand. "Lindy, you should not have come."

"Yeah, well, I have news that you may be interested in hearing," I said, turning my face up in his direction. "If I decide to do something, then I'm darn-well going to do it."

"I don't think you know what you are getting yourself into."

"Well, if that isn't the understatement of the century," I muttered. "Listen, I'm going to be part of this meeting with or without you." I started making confident strides forward.

Onn sighed and then rested his hand on my arm.

"Will you let go?" I attempted to wrench my arm from his grasp but without success. "I don't know who you think you are, but I don't need your guidance."

"It's a trapdoor, but let me know if you change your mind about needing my guidance." His hand released its grasp on my arm, and he disappeared as well.

I set my jaw in instant regret. I dragged the ground with my right foot; the opening was about a foot in front of me. I dropped to my hands and knees and felt around the opening for the ladder. It didn't take long to find it, and I slowly backed down and gingerly placed one foot on the first ladder rung while still holding onto the ground in front of me. Then I eased my way down the rungs. The others were arguing, but I didn't hear Onn. Magoumi was telling her version of how she found me. There were roars of laughter. I moved more quickly down the ladder, and my foot missed, and I started to fall backward with my leg caught between the rungs.

Then a pair of brawny arms caught me in an unintentional trust fall. "Do you still prefer to do this on your own?" That smug smirk still rang in Onn's voice.

"Just get me down."

CHAPTER 20

I T WAS THE SAME AS anywhere else in the Shadow Land, except maybe it was a little musty. I sat with my back against a clay wall and missed the coolness of the metal homes.

"Alright, Onn, who is she, and what is she carrying around?"

"I told you, Daveechi brought her here. She is fine."

Am I the only one who ran into those two on the way here?

"You always have so much faith in Daveechi." Avis was beside me, and his voice was loud in my ear. "Isn't that why we formed this group?"

"Simmer down, Avis," Deem said, "We all believe in the same cause. Daveechi is prolonging things unnecessarily. We've said from the beginning, all we are doing here is trying to give the resistance a kick-start."

"Okay, why is no one answering my question? That girl has something. She hit me with it."

"Listen!" Onn's voice commanded everyone's attention, "Lindy is in my care. If I say she is good, then she's good."

"I agree with Onn," Deem said, "I think we need to welcome our recruit."

I cleared my throat, "Thanks, Deem. I would like to make one thing clear: my name is Melinda." I had everyone's silent attention, "and that is all."

"You know about the resistance, don't you?" Magoumi asked.

"I know what Daveechi has told me about the tyrant," I said.

"Ha. Daveechi." Avis spat the words out like venom.

"Avis, Daveechi only does what he thinks is right."

"Does he, Onn? Does he?" Avis was moving away from me now and toward Onn, "If he is doing what is best for our people, then why are we still living like cowards in the dark, generation after generation."

"He's cautious, Av," Deem said.

"Yeah, well, something has got to be done," Avis turned back to me, "and that is why we are here, Soli. We are here to begin the war."

"The war has been raging for centuries, you glop," Magoumi said.

"Well, we have certainly been losing the war for centuries," Onn said. "I agree it is time we make a move."

"That's why I've got a plan."

Deem let out a long yawn and nudged me with his elbow. "And that is all we do down here, Soli, talk about what Daveechi isn't doing, talk about how we are going to do something, then we go home until the next meeting."

"Actually," I said, "I may have some information for you."

The stunned silence didn't last long as Avis scooted closer. "That's right! You should have to prove your worth to be admitted to this council."

"Lindy, what are you talking about?" Onn asked in a warning tone.

I drew in a long breath and continued, "On my way here, I overheard a conversation." The smell of *food* was on their breath as they all leaned in.

Everyone started talking at once.

"A conversation?" Onn repeated.

"No one is on the streets this late but us!" Avis spouted.

"See, she's pulling her weight," Deem said lazily.

"What was said?" Magoumi demanded.

"I honestly don't remember much of it, but I remember *who* was speaking."

"And?" Avis said.

"Daveechi . . . I think . . . and Jay Swartzentruber."

Everyone collectively slumped back—the hot breath was no longer in my face.

"Who's Jay Swartzentruber?" Deem said.

"He was the main reason I am here! He was trying to kill me and chased me into this world."

"Okay, but you are new here, Lindy. You're not used to life in the dark. Can you be certain it was Daveechi and this Jay person?" Onn questioned.

"Of course! I mean, maybe."

"Even if it was who she thinks it was, why should we care about some guy named Jay Swartzentruber?" Avis asked.

"Did you miss the part where he tried to kill me?"

"I just met you, Soli. It is a little early to make your enemy my enemy."

"What did they say?" Magoumi asked.

"Right. The two of them were talking about . . . " I tried to remember what they were saying. My mind went back to the moment: sitting on the ground, pressing up against the wall, trying not to breathe. "Um, well, Daveechi said he was protecting everyone, but Swartz didn't think that was good enough."

"Is that it?" Magoumi said.

"It wasn't so much what they said, but the *way* they said it, "I wished Onn would jump in and help me at this moment, "you know . . . sneakily?"

"So that's all you got? Our leader telling some guy we don't know that he wants to protect us, 'sneakily'?" Magoumi said, "It sounds like your friend got spooked in the dark, Onn."

"Listen, I've had about enough. If you have a problem with me, then you need to—"

"What's Soli like?" Deem interrupted.

"Are you kidding me, Deem?" Avis asked. "I mean, have you been paying any attention? We need to get more details out of her and scrutinize the likelihood of her story!"

"Eh, Magoumi is right, she got spooked while she was lost in the dark, but it's a once in a lifetime chance to get to talk to a Soli."

"Why don't you tell us about it, Lindy," Onn said.

I raised my eyebrows, trying to decide where to begin. "Okay. Well, you can see for one thing, and the light doesn't hurt at all. Ummm . . ." *How to explain?* "Everything that you all are afraid of or that hurts here is *good* in Soli. We go swimming for fun, pick flowers, and lay on a blanket right out in the grass. Being in the dark all the time would be depressing. And the food! There different types of food, and you can eat them fresh—straight from the garden is the best."

"See. That is why we are doing this. It's time. We need to take some action, and that will be our normal too!"

"Ok, Avis, you are going to scare Lindy," Onn said.

"I'm fine." I was getting more annoyed by this protective role Onn had given himself.

"She knows she can't tell anyone about this, right?" Deem asked.

"I won't tell," I said resolutely. If I ever wanted to get home, I needed to stay on everyone's good side.

"We have a recruit." Deem said with enthusiasm.

"I don't trust a Soli," Magoumi said.

I tilted my head and kept from speaking my mind, "I've already brought you some valuable information."

"Ha. That's debatable."

"Oh, come on, Magoumi; I say, a recruit is a recruit. Onn vouches for her, that's all I need," Deem said.

"I agree with Deem," Avis seconded.

"You three are all fools."

"Alright, I've got to get her back before someone notices she's gone," Onn said. "Let's go, Lindy."

"Ha. Nice try, Onn." Magoumi scoffed. "You think I would forget about whatever secret weapon your friend is toting around?"

Onn stood up, and he tugged on my arm to do the same, "Well, we got to go, so you are going to have to wait until next week's meeting to hear any more from our newest recruit."

I stretched out my hand for the rough ladder and began climbing out of the pit of darkness into another layer of darkness.

Onn walked behind me the whole way, and I gave him the silent treatment, although he didn't seem to mind. Finally, Onn nudged me to turn into the now-familiar doorway.

"Ah, home at last. Did you enjoy your evening stroll?" Di-ume's booming voice greeted us.

CHAPTER 21

"**F**ATHER, I CAN EXPL—"

"You will explain nothing!" Diume took a heavy step forward, and I stepped quickly to the wall and slid slowly toward my bed. Perhaps he would not know I had been part of this.

"Onn," Oi-u's voice quivered, "You know what happens if they catch you out on the streets past this hour?"

"Forget the guard! Do you know what is going to happen now that I have caught you!"

"Diume . . . " Oi-u's voice softly chided.

"Well? Are you going to explain yourself? What were you and the girl doing sneaking around?" Diume demanded.

Dagnabit.

"Father—"

"I sleepwalk."

Diume and Oi-u turned toward me in surprise.

I, I sleepwalk." I stammered. I sensed everyone waiting for me to continue. "It's a problem. Onn noticed I was gone and went out to rescue me." Still, no one spoke. "I mean, it took a while for me to wake up, which is why—"

"Yes," Onn interrupted, "Yes, I was watching out for her . . . like you asked."

Diume grunted, "Well, now you can do your part by sleeping at night and doing honest work during the day." He walked away,

"I will be vigilant. We wouldn't want something like this to happen again, would we?"

"No, Father."

After that, Diume slept in the doorway every night. The midnight meetings came to a screeching halt.

CHAPTER 22

"**G**OOD MORNING, ALL!" DAVEECHI'S CHEERY voice woke me. "And how are we on this fine day?"

I rolled over and groaned.

"Hmm, still in bed, I take it." Daveechi didn't sound pleased, "Well, it is time to be off."

"Off where?" Diume was already up and about.

Daveechi turned to Onn. "You must take Melinda to Knowledge Square. She has much to learn if she is going to be of any use to us."

"But Daveechi, she will need—"

"Yes, she shall have to start at Square One," Daveechi said.

"But Daveechi—"

"Hup—" Daveechi interrupted and said firmly, "The Soli knows nothing of our land or our customs. Melinda, are you still in bed? Come now, we've got much to accomplish and not much time to do it." And with that, he was gone.

I stretched and let out a long yawn and rested my hand on the satchel, which still held the cursed fiddle. I had flung it over the edge of the round pillow bed and had gained some relief from the dull pain it beamed onto my side and arm. Now it slung down by my side once more. How much longer until I get rid of it and go home? *What I would give for a burger.*

Onn pushed me toward the door, and as we were leaving, Oi-u whispered to Onn, "Be careful." I was sure Diume was glaring at us as we went.

I waited until we had walked several squares before I ventured to speak. "Onn, what are we going to do?"

"Hush," he said. The bustle of the Shadow Village surrounded us.

"But we're going tonight, remember?"

"Do you wish to expose us to the village?" Onn said in an angry whisper, "We will find a way."

I rubbed the lingering sleep out of my eyes. "Where are we going anyway?"

Onn gently tugged my hand. I was lumbering behind. "Daveechi enrolled you in the Knowledge Square."

"School?" I groaned. "I have a major case of senioritis as it is."

"Yeah, well, you better get over that."

We walked in silence for the rest of the way, but soon the chatter of Square One approached and, soon after, a powerful stench.

"No way, I ain't gonna go nowhere that smells like that!"

"Daveechi's orders."

"Ain't no way," I repeated.

"It's a bunch of shadlings. Where there are a bunch of shadlings together, there are bound to be some interesting smells.

"Shadlings?"

We neared the entrance, and I put my hand over the satchel.

"I'll come by to get you after work," Onn said as he released his grip on my hand.

"Don't you dare leave me here. Onn!"

"Alright," a nasal voice rose above the rest, "settle down and find a seat."

Students found seats, and there was a clatter like someone had tripped over a desk.

"Melinda?"

"Um, present?"

The nasal voice continued, "Have you found a seat?"

"Not exactly, no."

"Come."

A rounded wooden stick was placed in my hand, and it pulled me forward and stopped when I arrived at a desk.

"Sit," said the nasal voice.

I reached my hand out and slid into my seat; however, as I did, my hand slid across the table and into a cold and sticky blob. "Yuuahhh!" I leaped back out of the chair, wiping my hand furiously on my pants. "It's a loogie!" I shouted.

The room exploded with childish giggles.

"Silence!" The voice became even more nasal than before.

"Yes, Sir!" I roared, still standing beside my seat.

"Madam," the voice wheezed, "I am Madam Wai."

"Oh, I—I'm so sorry."

"Now, Melinda, you are the oldest student here and have caused the most disruption. Can we sit in our seat and not cause a scene?"

"Oldest student here?"

A teeter of giggles erupted around me.

"Kindly take your seat. Now, as I was saying—"

"Madam?"

The teacher let out a long exasperated sigh. "Yyyesss?"

"Can I—er—May I have another seat? I can't—I just can't."

"Find a seat quickly and be silent!" The teacher was nearly yelling at me but still coated it with a sing-song in her voice.

I hurried to the row behind me and sat down hurriedly; however, as I did, a small yelp informed me I had not chosen wisely.

"Madam!" A voice gasped from beneath me. "She's smooshing me!"

"Melinda," the voice broke out of its sugar coating for just a moment before glazing back into the sing-song, "please choose a seat that is not already occupied."

"No offense, but I don't see how I am supposed to do that when I barely have any idea where the seats *are,* much less if some kid is sitting there wiping nasty boogers over everything."

Another long sigh. "If you would get your bottom into a seat, you might learn something about that."

I reached out, cautiously feeling my way down the row of desks until I found an empty seat. Madam continued teaching her lesson.

"Now, shadlings, please take out your text-o-boards."

I raised my hand out of years of habit, then, realizing this was useless, said, "Madam?"

"Your text-o-board is in front of you on your desk, Melinda."

I slid my hand out, barely touching the desk in front of me for fear of another surprise. A wooden board was indeed on my desk. It was about a foot in both width and height. On the board were rows of different shapes. There were about ten shapes in each row and five rows. Each shape had a different texture or pattern.

"Ok, everyone, we shall recite our signs. Put your finger on sign one!"

"Hold up," I said. "Where is sign one?"

Another sigh. "Well, where do you think sign one would be located, darling?"

"I mean, my guess would be the top left corner."

"Very good. Ok, fingers ready!"

The entire class chanted, and I suppose they were moving along the shapes. I tried to keep up, but before long, I was behind. My fingers slid over the shape. The first one was a square. It was completely smooth; the next was a circle with raised slants through it. Others were polka-dotted, striped, rectangles, triangles, some were raised, and others were indented.

"Madam! I am lost."

"Melinda, try your best to keep up, Road, River . . . "

"Could you maybe—hey! Madam, one of your hoodlums is poking me."

" . . . home, food, I think you can handle it Melinda, clothing, drink . . . "

I tried to swat at the finger, but I missed, and the little guy moved to my back. Pretty soon, there were two, then three fingers poking me.

"Madam, more of them are doing it!"

"—path, Upperlands—fingers on your boards—bed, door . . . "

"Whaaooohwwet willy! Someone gave me a wet willy!" I jumped out of my seat and hopped up and down as I wiped my saliva covered ear on my shoulder, "Can you please control your children."

A hand clutched my upper arm, and I was being pushed back into my seat. "I will have no more outburst from you, Melinda. Silence, Tavis, or I am coming over there next! Melinda put your finger on the board, and I do not want to hear another word out of you!"

Madam continued leading the class in reciting the signs, and I sat stunned in my seat for all of thirty seconds. Then I stood up. "Madam, I'm sorry, but I am a new student here, and not only that, I'm from another world!" The class went silent—all ears were on me. "I mean, c'mon, they sent me to this school to learn. Weeeeellll, let me tell you what I've learned so far: First, I was shoved in here with no direction, made fun of for not magically finding my seat in the dark, your children are wild and out of control, and I know absolutely nothing about your world or its systems, yet you are doing nothing to help me learn it! You tell me, Madam, what kind of school is this?"

CHAPTER 23

"MADAM WAI BELIEVES MELINDA WOULD be better placed under a private tutor," Daveechi said to Diume. Daveechi had popped by for dinner and brought this mouthful to us, "She says that Melinda needs an approach that is much more 'hands-on.'"

"Hands-on? Are you kidding me? Did that woman say "hands-on"?"

"Is there a problem with that, Melinda?" Diume asked.

"No, sir," Onn jumped in.

"Good!" Daveechi said, "Onn will be your tutor."

Oi-u took in a sharp breath. "Onn? Why Onn?"

"Well, he has done a fair job showing Melinda around the Shadow Village, has he not?"

"He has," Diume said dryly.

"Then it's settled."

"So it appears," Oi-u said.

"Hands-on," I muttered.

"Now, you will begin tomorrow." Daveechi said, "Onn, she needs a crash course."

"Aren't we doing this to avoid crashes?" I asked loud enough for only Onn to hear me. He didn't laugh.

Daveechi continued, "Get in the basics: teach her the signs, and how to navigate around the shadow village, and most importantly, how to navigate the Upperlands."

"Yes, sir, we can start right away."

"Right now?" I wanted to punch him. I had been through enough nonsense today.

"Well, you know, why wait?" Onn said, "We have a lot to cover."

"I like that attitude, Onn," Daveechi said, "Off to it, then!"

CHAPTER 24

A S SOON AS WE WERE out the door, I was dragged down the street. My hand was in Onn's, and my arm was wholly extended as Onn practically ran down the incline. "Onn!" I said with exasperation, "why are you going so fast?" I was being jostled around like a ball in a pinball machine—at midday, the streets were packed again.

"We're late!"

"Late? How can we be late for a private tutoring session? I am a fast learner, but this ain't gonna cut it!" My southern accent grew thicker as it tends to any time I am flustered, "Let me tell ya, those signs were hard enough to keep up with sitting down!"

Without responding, Onn whiplashed around a corner, and I swung around wildly, slamming into the ordinary walkers like they were bowling pins. "So sorry!" I called as I was whisked away. We were drawing attention, and Onn slowed his pace.

"I don't know what kind of lesson this is, but—"

"Silence," Onn said in a whisper.

The streets were quiet again, and I recognized the silence. The road was softer here, so even our steps were hushed. *We are going back.* My heart started racing as Onn's urgency now made sense. I was happy not to be left out this time. I determined to learn everything about this place if I was ever going to get out of this strange nightmare and back home. *This is my chance.*

I begrudgingly allowed Onn to help me down the trap door this time, and the murmur of voices continued as I climbed in, "Hello, y'all."

"Melinda!" Magoumi exclaimed. "She's supposed to be at Square One today."

"She has a new private tutor." Onn dropped beside me.

"What better place for a first lesson than our society of hooligans," Deem said in his usual carefree manner.

"I can't believe you are having this meeting in the middle of the day!" I said.

"Eh, in hindsight, it might be safer this way, anyway." Deem said.

"As long as no one realizes we're gone. It was lucky that Daveechi assigned me as Lindy's tutor; otherwise, I might never have gotten out of the house again."

"Will you all stop yammering and sit down!" Avis demanded.

I reached a hand out to the dusty wall behind me and slid down into a comfortable sitting position.

"Yeah, let's get this started. Lunch break doesn't last forever," Magoumi said.

"Alright, any new business?" Onn asked, still catching his breath.

"Overthrow Daveechi. Surge into war," Deem said in a mellow tone.

"This is not a joking matter, Deem," Magoumi said.

"Daveechi has us all around his finger, and we are living here like rats. We have to do something!" Avis said.

"Daveechi is only doing what he thinks is best," Onn said.

"Who made Daveechi king anyway?" I asked.

"He's not a king," Avis seethed.

"History. A lot of history," Onn said.

"Well, you *are* supposed to be tutoring her," Deem said.

"I'll tell her." Magoumi slid over to me.

I scooted back and huffed some hair out of my face to hide my annoyance that Magoumi would be the one to educate me.

"Long ago, when the world was first made, we did not have to live in the shadows," Magoumi said, "Chaira was like Soli. Everyone walked in the light and did as they pleased without fear of burning or suffering any pain, but the tyrant made our people serve him."

"We were slaves!" Avis interjected.

"Yes," Magoumi continued, "although we did not live in hiding or have to fear the burning, we were slaves destined to do only what the tyrant commanded. We did not know what life would be like outside the tyrant's reign. Our people even called him the great king, and we did his bidding blindly. Each of our shadow fathers had specific tasks and were assigned to a Hall in the tyrant's palace."

"Assigned to a Hall?" I asked, "What do you mean?"

"His palace is full of Halls: the Hall of Canvases, the Hall of Sculptures, the Hall of Electricities, the Hall of Ideas, and the Hall of Music. Everyone spent their days doing nothing but creating and envisioning ideas to add to the tyrant's domain. He made creatures stay in their halls and do their assigned duties. It kept the world moving and working to the tyrant's satisfaction."

"Isn't that kind of what y'all do down here with the factory squares?"

"We never do things like the tyrant!" Avis shouted. I grimaced and wiped spit particles from my face.

"Cool it, Avis," Onn said. "Freedom is the key here, not style."

"Didn't mean to offend," I muttered.

"Anyway," Magoumi continued, "Daveechi was there in the beginning. He used to oversee the Hall of Music. He wrote every song and arrangement to please the tyrant. Daveechi was the most talented artisan in all the tyrant's kingdom."

My hand slipped down to the still covered violin. *Was this one of Daveechi's masterpieces, and if so, why he didn't want it back?*

"Daveechi started to question the tyrant's motives. He then convinced two of his fellow craftworkers to rebel against the tyrant to rule themselves."

"What were their names?" I grabbed Magoumi's arm.

"What?"

"The two that Daveechi convinced to help. What were their names?"

"Well, I was getting to that." Magoumi wretched her arm away from me. "Odessa and Jael."

Odessa was an idea-creature. But she wanted more than anything to live and work as a musician . . . "

Magoumi continued to talk, but I did not hear her. *Shadow Creatures. Mrs. Aidan Odessa and Jay Swartzentruber are shadow creatures! How did they get into my world? How long had they been there? Why didn't they come back? Why did Odessa send me here? What would happen if I did not fulfill the job?* I became aware of Magoumi's voice once more as she continued the story.

"So, they broke into war to overthrow the king, but they completely underestimated his power. Daveechi escaped to the Shadowlands, and he rescued others and brought them with him. However, the tyrant banished Odessa and Jael from Chaira."

"Their effort accomplished nothing," I said to myself.

"Not quite," Onn said.

"Yes," Magoumi said, "Before they were banished to Soli, it is said that Odessa stole one instrument before she went—the violin."

"I don't understand. What does that have to do with the burning?" I asked.

Avis threw himself at this question. "Clearly, the tyrant would not allow half of his slave labor to go free with no retaliation. So, he told all the rest that we were banished and put this curse of burning onto us. All those that choose to return to him, he takes the burning away, and a fear of the burning keeps his slaves from leaving."

"Daveechi opened many eyes to see that the king is only a tyrant who has enslaved them. And while many choose to live in slavery to the tyrant, some follow Daveechi to begin the resistance," Onn said, leaning toward me.

"Ha. Begin the resistance." Deem said in a firm, sneering voice, uncharacteristic of him, "What has changed since then?"

"I agree we are moving slowly, but Daveechi has done much for us," Onn said, and his voice was tense.

"Really?" Avis was quick to join in. "What has he done for us, Onn? Build our people another prison; that is what he has done."

"You go too far, Avis," Onn said through his teeth.

"Onn, I agree with Avis, for once," Magoumi said. "Daveechi claims to be working to overthrow the tyrant, but we have been at a standstill since that first rebellion."

"Daveechi is the only one left who truly knows what we are dealing with!" Onn said.

"Odessa and Jay know, too," I said in a whisper.

"Well, a lot of good they can do for us. No word from them since the tyrant banished them," Onn said, sounding exasperated.

"*I* have spoken to them."

"You have what?" All of them turned their focus to me now.

"Yes," I stammered, "I mean, that is how I got here. Odessa, she sent me."

"That is why Daveechi takes an interest in you," Onn whispered.

"Magoumi, that thing that hit you, you remember? It is the violin. I mean *the violin*. Odessa sent me with strict instructions to return it to its place."

"Return it?" It was Onn who started at this. "That is madness! It would give the tyrant what he needed and give away our advantage!"

"Who told you that, Daveechi?" Avis sneered.

"He didn't have to; it is common sense! The thing needs to be destroyed—that should be our move," Onn said.

"Actually, I was on my way to do what Odessa said, and it was Daveechi who told me to destroy the fiddle."

"Onn, you got to admit, there hasn't been much progress since that first rebellion. Maybe it's time to try something new. Odessa is as capable as Daveechi."

"Odessa is not part of this world anymore. Nor will she ever be again. She can't know what the world is like now, and she will not be around for whatever consequences incur from her plans." Onn was standing now.

"Jay tried to stop me from carrying out Odessa's plan. I figured, you know, he was a creep, but there's always the possibility he knew what he was talking about."

Onn's affirming hand came down on my shoulder. "Daveechi has been with us through it all, and he knows whatever decisions he makes will affect him as well as everyone else." Onn paused, and no one else spoke. "When I started this group, it was never to rebel against Daveechi. It was to help the cause. You all have taken it too far," emotion was building in his voice, "I can no longer be a part of this."

"Onn," Deem pleaded, "we are ready to enact the plan!"

"We are not ready, Deem, as I have told you again and again. That is my last request: please do not carry out the plan until you are more in number."

"We can get the numbers, Onn. You are the one holding us back from that as well," Avis stormed.

"Let's go, Lindy." His hand slid into mine and pulled me toward the ladder.

I paused. The fiddle's heat was slowly creating a deeper burn in my side. It was unbearable. I internally tried to reason through the best and fastest way to get home.

Onn must have sensed my hesitancy. "Lindy?"

I shook my head slowly. "I'm staying here, Onn."

Onn didn't say a word. His grip went limp, and my hand dropped to my side. Angry steps sounded on the ladder and then quiet.

CHAPTER 25

"ONN YOU CAN'T WALK OUT on this!" Magoumi yelled after him.

Avis pounded his fist into the wall, and brittle clay pieces fell onto my shoulder and hair.

Deem sighed. "We don't have time to talk about it now. I've got to get back to work."

"Meeting tonight at the regular time. I'll talk to Onn later," Magoumi said. "Melinda, come on, I'll take you back. I'm late to work all the time."

Still unsure about what had happened and what the repercussions of my hasty decisions might be, I followed Magoumi obediently.

We were soon back on the bustling streets. "We better teach you a little before you get back if you were supposed to be in a tutoring session." Magoumi said absently, "What are you supposed to be studying?"

"Signs."

"Oh, that's easy." She grabbed my wrist and hoicked me to the side of the road, pressing my hand on the corner of one of the cold metal homes. One of the textured signs was under my fingertips. "On every square corner are at least two signs." Magoumi shifted my fingers up. It was a smooth square. "This one simply means housing squares. Factory squares have raised slants." She moved my hand down to the first sign. It was a circle with three indented circles. It was like rubbing my fingers over a domino. "This means we are in Venn Square. Every square has its sign on each corner."

"I will never remember all this," I said.

"You will, with practice. Memorize the outer squares first and then work your way in and learn the sign for your square. Each house has a certain number of slashes. Diume's home is on River square slash three. Eight homes per square."

We walked on, Magoumi showing me each square's sign, and I distractedly listened as she explained the system.

"Here we are, River Square." I reached my hand out to the corner and brushed my fingers over the sign—the smooth square and the three waves. *River Square.*

"Remember, slash three," Magoumi reminded, "Do you remember how to get back to the meeting?"

"Yes, from River Square to slash one, Fay Square to Quart Square slash four, to um—"

"Lew Slash eight," Magoumi prompted.

"Right, Lew Square slash eight, to Venn Square slash five, and the outer wall."

Magoumi must have been satisfied because she pushed me forward toward Diume's home.

"Thank you, Magoumi."

"See you tonight," she lingered to make sure I found the correct door frame. The first one—six slashes. I walked past it; my toes curled around the quarter studded path. *Seven, ah eight.* I slid into the door frame.

Someone said my name in a familiar, deep voice.

"So, Melinda is taking private lessons," Jay said.

Diume's voice thundered, "Of course, much more efficient that way, don't you think?"

"How do you like hosting the girl? I would think she would be a tremendous burden to you."

"Not at all."

I scowled in the darkness at him and muttered, "It's funny how, when the host doesn't terrorize his guests, they become so much less burdensome." Before anyone had a chance to respond, someone swung into the doorway, slamming into me.

"So sorry!" It was Daveechi. "I didn't realize someone was in the door. People don't generally stand in doorways."

"Who is in the door?" Diume boomed.

"Sorry, sorry," I said, rubbing my elbow. "It's me, Melinda."

"How long were you standing there?" Jay questioned.

"And where is Onn?" Oi-u spoke up.

"Well, um, he sent me home to test my newly learned skills, and he is an excellent teacher," I chuckled nervously, "because I made it."

"Hmmm," Diume did not seem convinced.

"Melinda, this is Jael, as you may recall. As luck would have it, he has agreed to help us with our endeavors!"

I shook my head. "I will not agree to help him."

"Why, Melinda, why would you refuse help like that?" Daveechi asked.

"You, of all people, should understand. This man was trying to kill me!"

"And yet, you would not let him die but saved him."

"Well, clearly, I made a mistake."

"Firstly, I did not try to kill you. I only wanted to stop you from taking that blasted instrument back to the tyrant. Odessa is a fool. She regrets her ways and would undo all that we've worked so hard for!"

"Not now, Jael," Daveechi said. He then continued in a cheerier voice, "I've just dropped by to see how tutoring was coming along, and it seems to be going well, so I better get back to work. Jael, are you heading back too? I'll walk with you."

"Right, nice talking with you, Diume, Oi-u. I'll see you later."

"Same, of course, Jael."

The two of them left hastily, and I gritted my teeth, all the more determined to escape this world.

CHAPTER 26

ONN ARRIVED HOME IN TIME for dinner, and I did not get a chance to talk to him. He did not make any effort to speak to me either.

I helped Oi-u clean up and then collapsed in bed. Onn still did not say a word to me. I hated that he was mad at me. After all, Onn had been there for me since I first came to the Shadow Village. He had been a better friend to me than Daveechi, but I had to get home, and if it came down to protecting me or protecting his country, Onn would undoubtedly choose the latter without flinching.

I laid awake that night, trying to decide if I should go to the meeting. Should I wake Onn and take him with me? All the others were against him now, and he was so angry at them; it might blow up again, and the rest of them might be another obstacle standing in my way. He might even keep me from going at all. *I have to talk to them. Maybe they can help me get out of here in exchange for the fiddle. Even if they don't, they don't care enough to stop me.*

Getting out of the house was the first hurdle. Diume's light snoring signaled he was still in his place directly in the doorway. I slipped out of my bed, feet first, and cautiously tapped the pathway with my toes. I found it and lifted myself from the bed. It made barely any sound, but even the quietest sounds become firecrackers when sneaking around. One step at a time. *Where is the table? I cannot run into that.* I reached my hand out and found it jutting ever-so-slightly into my path. I slid my hand out over it to make sure no stray dishes remained to signal my presence.

Once I made it past the table, I crept over to the wall, as not to run into any unexpected obstacles. I pressed my back against the cold metal frame and slid sideways toward the door frame. A light scraping sound was the result, and I quickly stopped moving. The snoring turned to gentle breathing, and the stillness that resulted was unnerving. I slid across the metal wall at a softer pace. Finally, I stopped. Diume's warm breath breezed over my toes.

I placed my hands on either side of the door frame and stood leaning over Diume, who I envisioned as a ferocious sleeping beast guarding the entrance. I lifted my foot almost to my chin in a giant step to avoid stepping on him and placed it on the safety of the quiet street. I was now standing one foot inside the house and one foot on the road. It was at this moment Diume rolled over. Like a lumbering bear deep in hibernation, he turned slowly with something like a growl, and I froze in panic as the monstrous head came to rest on my toes. My entire left foot was buried under a tangle of beard and hair. I now stood like a statue in a lunge pose. Both of my arms froze in midair, and I dared not move a muscle. *What do I do? What can I do? I have to do something!* The light snoring continued. I eased my foot out from under him, but as soon as I did, Diume snorted and shifted further onto my foot.

"Who's there?" His gruff voice said, still from within sleep. I stopped moving and tried to stop breathing. The gentle snoring picked back up again as he drifted back into sleep. I put my hands to my face. *New plan. New plan.*

A hushed voice spoke only a few inches from my face. "Diume?"

Daveechi. I didn't hear his footsteps.

"Diume, I have urgent news I must discuss with you."

Diume sat bolt upright, hitting his head on my knee and simultaneously releasing my foot, sending me sprawling forward into Daveechi's leg and then onto the footpath beyond. *Dead. Dead. I'm dead.* Now I was caught by both Diume and Daveechi.

"Daveechi! What do you mean coming at this hour and waking me up in this way! I will have a headache for the rest of the night!"

"I'm sorry, my friend, but it is urgent, and your head has not done my leg any favors either."

I slammed into both of them, but they each think it was the other. I held in a cackle.

"What in all that is darkness is urgent enough to wake me at this hour?"

"Not here, come inside."

Diume rose, with much grunting and growling, from the threshold, and Daveechi entered, talking as he went, "It has come to my attention that a band of youngsters is attempting to begin . . . " His voice faded as they left the entrance. I considered staying to hear what he said, but my heart was still beating rapidly from my narrow escape. *I'm already late for the meeting.*

Toes gripping the walk, I made my way down the incline, feeling for signs. I had been repeating the order of signs to myself all day. "River Square to slash one Fay Square to Quart Square slash four, to Lew Square slash eight, to Venn Square slash five, and the outer wall," I muttered over and over. My hands shook as I reached out for each sign. One more square. My fingers brushed over the smooth square and the accompanying circle with the three dots. *Venn Square. One, two, three, four, five, slashes.*

I was outside the village now. With no one there to lead me, I was terrified I would fall through the trapdoor. I inched forward—feeling the soft dirt with my bare toes until it turned into wood. *This was it.* I tapped my foot on the wooden floor door a few times to be sure. *I made it.* I pumped my fist into the dark.

The trap door let out a high-pitched squeak as I slowly opened it. I let myself down tenderly on the ladder, feeling safe at last. "It's me! Melinda," I said, relief flooding into my voice.

"You made it!" Deem said enthusiastically.

"Well done," Magoumi said.

The ladder creaked behind me. "I still don't know why I got babysitting duty."

"Shut up, Avis," Magoumi said.

"Babysitting duty?" I questioned, "Were you following me?"

"We wanted to make sure you got here in one piece."

I pursed my lips but didn't say anything.

"I have to say, you pulled quite the trick on Daveechi and Diume."

"You followed me the whole way?"

"You tricked Daveechi and Diume?" Magoumi asked, "That's risky. Diume is one of Daveechi's best men."

I rubbed the back of my neck. "Well, it was luck, really."

"What are we going to do about Onn?" Avis asked pointedly, "Has anyone talked to him?"

"He wouldn't say a word to me," I said.

"We need to forget about Onn." Magoumi said fiercely, "He was holding us back anyway."

"So then, we carry on with the plan." Deem spoke so softly I wasn't sure it was him talking.

"Yes!" Avis said, "I say yes, and I think we should do it at our first opportunity. The next time the tyrant sends a message."

"Wait, the tyrant sends messages?" I asked with surprise.

Magoumi slumped down on the ground beside me and tugged at me to do the same. "You should tell us more about you and your life. You didn't get to say much before."

"Isn't there more important stuff to talk about right now?"

"We need some motivation right now."

"Okay." I paused, wondering when I should bring up my trade idea. "Well, like I said, pretty much everything bad here is good in my world. For example, even this instrument," I set my hand on the violin, and it still was like holding my hand over a stove burner, "before I came here, I actually admired this violin. I was amazed by how beautiful it was." I laughed lightly, "In fact, this all started because I couldn't resist picking it up and plucking the strings a little."

A collective gasp burst from the group.

"Yeah, yeah, I'm sure that sounds crazy here, but back there . . . " I sighed. How to explain to these shadow creatures what it is like to live, unafraid and unhurt, in the light. Music. There hadn't been a single note since I'd arrived. It was such a massive part of my world. I took a breath and began to sing, barely above a whisper, the first song that came to my mind—an old hymn from my childhood:

> My heart has no desire to stay
> Where doubts arise and fears dismay;
> Though some may dwell where these abound,
> My prayer, my aim, is higher ground.[1]

Almost as soon as I began to sing, the three of them shouted wildly at me to stop. I was confused by this, as I have been told I have a lovely singing voice, but the confusion did not last long. Before my voice echoed off the small hovel's walls, the ground started shaking.

"Out! Everyone out!" Avis was shouting.

Dirt and rocks were falling all around us. Bodies jostled me as the three of them rushed to the ladder. The air was filled with dry dust as the roof and walls collapsed. I started coughing uncontrollably as I tried to find the ladder. I held one hand out, searching for the first rung, and the other I used to shield my head and face from the debris falling all around.

"Help!" I choked, "Magoumi, wait, please, help me!"

"Melinda! Over here!"

I turned toward her voice and tried to move forward faster.

"Hurry, Melinda, it is going to cave in!" Now her voice was coming from the other direction.

I spun around. "Help me!" Something knocked into my head, and I fell to the ground. A flood of dirt slid over my legs, and I was buried up to my waist. I was coughing even harder now and trying franticly to pull myself out of the sand trap. More rocks pelted me from above. I covered my head with both my arms and laid my head down in the dirt.

"Melinda!" It was Avis.

---

1. Johnson Oatman, Jr.. *Higher Ground.* hymnary.org

"Here!" I wheezed, "I'm over here." Soon after, a pair of hands were on my dust-plated arm.

"I've got her," Avis shouted. He pulled me out of my shallow grave. Deem and Magoumi yelled directions to guide us to the ladder.

"You shouldn't have come back. There's no way we're going to make it out of here in time."

"Come on!" Avis said as he yanked me toward the voices.

Deem and Magoumi's voices grew closer and more distinct. *We are going to make it.* Their voices rang right above us.

"No!" Avis released my arm. "No, it's gone! The ladder is gone." My heart dropped. A landslide roared in behind us. *The ceiling is collapsing.*

"Where? Where is it?" Magoumi screamed.

"Buried." Avis didn't say this loud enough for Magoumi and Deem to hear.

"Here!" It was Deem's voice. He was right in front of me. "Here!" He kept repeating, and fingertips brushed my forehead. I reached out, and his hand slapped my arm as it waved past me again. Avis caught on before I did, and he kicked my shoulder as I guessed he must be climbing up Deem like a rope. I was right behind him. I'm sure I used Deem's head as a foothold as I frantically climbed up, hearing the roar of the rest of the hovel collapsing in behind us. Avis and Magoumi were pulling me out, and then I turned and began pulling Deem up with them by his feet. He came out making gasping and sputtering sounds as if from underwater.

The air was dusty but silent once again. I reached my foot out cautiously. The opening was filled in with dirt. The secret hideout must be nothing more than a pit in the darkness now.

"I—I don't know what to say—"

"Whatever you do, don't sing it." Deem said warily.

"I'm so sorry, I had no idea."

"I'm glad everyone is okay," Avis said softly.

"Yes," Magoumi agreed.

"Thank you. Thank you for coming back for me." I said, "I owe you all my life."

"Well," Avis said, "then there is something you can help us with."

CHAPTER 27

I SLIPPED INTO MY BED UNDETECTED. Diume no longer guarded the entry, which was good since I was still shaken from nearly being buried alive. I don't know if I was steady enough to sneak past him again. I lay awake for hours thinking about what to do. Avis had laid out the plan. I had to help them, didn't I?

Soon Oi-u's quiet stirring signaled the day was beginning. Onn acted as if nothing had happened between us. We ate our food as usual, and the family chatted idly. I had half expected Diume to confront me about our run in last night, but he was none the wiser.

"Ready, Lindy?"

I jumped. *Did he know?* "Ready? For what?" I asked.

"Your tutoring session. What else?"

Diume was preparing for a day of work. "Be careful, you two. Stay out of trouble."

I walked without Onn holding my hand today. I did not need it, and he did not offer it. His steps continued in their usual rhythm. Ours were the only footsteps on the path now, with only a few Shaddians still plodding off to work.

"Onn?"

"Lindy?" He said, keeping his pace in front of me.

"Have you ever been, you know, above?"

"No," he said shortly.

My hand brushed over a break in the smooth wall. "Oh." I tried again, "Onn, if you have never been, how will you know what to do when the time comes to battle?"

"You know how all the villagers learn how to navigate the grid?" The intensity eased out of his tone.

"Yes, of course."

"Well, in the same way, we are also taught to navigate the world above."

"So even though you've never been there, you can get around with your eyes shut," I chuckled to myself.

Onn didn't laugh. "I will someday."

"When your people defeat the tyrant?" I asked in a tone that matched his.

"I will go before that. It is untelling if we will ever overthrow the tyrant."

"But I—"

"The others are right. Daveechi spins his tales to give hope. My father—" His steps faltered now, "My father has served him his whole life."

"To defy Daveechi would be to defy your dad," I said, nodding. I reached forward and attempted to hold his hand, but he continued talking and, in doing so, waved his hand forward. *Ha. He talks with his hands.*

"Daveechi will tell us whatever he needs to keep spirits up and make us believe we have the upper hand." He lowered his voice as we moved over to allow other travelers to pass. "The truth is, if we are doing so well in this battle, we wouldn't be living in this quarry for generations."

His frank manner stunned me. The violin chafed at my leg; I was sure the satchel was wearing thin. "So, you agree with Avis and the rest?" I said, pondering if I should tell him of last night's happenings.

"We need change, but we need to be smart."

"Onn," I ventured cautiously, "Have you ever seen yourself?"

Onn paused, "I have never seen my face." The incline was steeper now. "But I have seen my hands."

"Your hands? How?"

"The light came to us."

I tried to understand what this meant. Why were Onn and the others so dissatisfied with the village? After my experience with their Upperlands, I would never want to go back unless it was to get home. Sure, the Shadowlands were not the best, but it was safe from the pains and terrors of the light and the tyrant. What more did he want?

"What about you?"

"What about me?" I asked.

"What do you look like?"

"Well, I mean, I'm—" I let out a quick sigh. *How to explain?* "I have long black hair—it is the color of, you know, the darkness, but my skin—it is more like the light."

Onn gasped at this.

"No, I mean in color. I am pale, with, um, darker spots scattered all over my face and arms—those are called freckles, and um, I mean—"

"Are you beautiful?"

I grew embarrassed. "I don't know, I guess."

"They say the tyrant's lands are beautiful. What does beautiful look like?"

"Isn't anything from the tyrant revolting?"

Onn didn't answer, but he stopped abruptly, and I fell into him. Onn reached for my hand, and I did not pull away.

Pain pierced my side before the actual flash. The pain distracted me, and I did not see what caused the flash or from where it came. The sudden light blinded me more than the darkness. Onn hurled me into a ditch and pulled a thick blanket around us that blocked out the light. He must be well-practiced in the maneuver because I didn't get a glimpse of what was going on. The melodic voice of a shining one echoed through the air, although my panic kept me from understanding the words it spoke. "What is going on?" I demanded in a raspy whisper.

Onn's voice did not seem alarmed, "It is only a message from the tyrant to entice anyone who will to join his ranks."

"Join the tyrant?" I clenched my teeth. "How can it even get down here?" The violin was blazing a hole through my skin.

"They can come anywhere. The tyrant has no limits. Though we usually ward them off."

"Has anyone joined?" I asked.

"Some."

"What becomes of them?"

"The tyrant persuades them to come to him, but anyone who comes will be no more."

"No more?"

Onn shifted his weight, and his breath was on my face. "Don't you ever wonder where the light comes from? It is the tyrant. He is the source of the light. When the shining ones bring recruits before him, they are no more. They disappear in his presence."

"Why?"

"To weaken our forces," Onn's voice was dry, and he rolled onto his back.

The pain was becoming unbearable. I slid my hand between the satchel and my ribs, half expecting to find my skin rubbed raw. But it was smooth. Then I had a realization. I was looking at the blanket ceiling. At that moment, Onn must have seen it too. He let out a short yelp and lunged out from under the cover. The golden voice of the shining one continued to ring, and the soft glow exuding from my satchel was growing brighter.

I was no longer used to the harshness of the light, and all I wanted to do was get away from it. So, I left the fiddle for the first time since I had come to this strange world. I stopped, dropped, and rolled out of the shelter, leaving the violin still tucked away so that only faint grayness stood out in the black of the village.

A mutter of voices surrounded me. *Where was Onn?*

The village was empty. I assumed the shadow creatures were still hiding beneath the canvases. *They must have drills for this or something.* The brightness of the shining one lit up the whole Shadow Village. Everything was visible now, though still cloaked in shadows. I ducked behind one of the homes. The metal sides were painted black and didn't reflect light. High on a slope outside the village stood the shining one, spouting off the same message as always.

Then, as I watched all this, something even more astonishing appeared. Three figures, like puny shadows compared to the shining one, were creeping up behind it with weapons in hand. One was in the front, and the other two followed behind. The two in the back had a sword in one hand and a dagger in the other, but the one on front carried a long whip. *It must be time.* My breath faltered. I had to decide; I had to choose now. *I can't do it.* A hand gripped my forearm. I tried to tear away, but the hand held on firmly. I bit my lip to keep myself from crying out. It was Onn. He stood stoically behind me, and his hand slipped into mine.

"The fools," he whispered hoarsely in my ear, and tears were in his voice. Onn released my hand, and his figure darted past me. The others were several squares away, but he sprinted toward them. I stood rooted to the road—unable to look away—unable to follow.

The three were nearing the shining one. The one in front, who I assumed to be Magoumi, was so close she could have reached out and touched it. It was growing harder and harder to see them as they grew thin from the light, as I had when I first entered this world. Then, Avis shouted a battle cry, and the three leaped onto the shining one.

"For Victory!" And Onn's voice echoed the cry. He would not make it in time.

All three vanished before they even landed a blow. Not one of them reached the shining one. They were gone. I drew in a sharp breath. The shining one retreated, and everything was dark once again. Tears sprung in my eyes. *Gone.* Awash of guilt came over me. Still, I stayed rooted to the same spot in the road, staring into the darkness and feeling the weight of my choice.

Slowly, the town came back to life. Shadow creatures crept out from under the tarps and back into the streets. Confusion was everywhere. *Was Onn gone too?* Voices around me were plotting what to do to the shining one who brought the torch of the tyrant. Had anyone else even seen what had happened?

Something grabbed my arm in the darkness. It wasn't Onn. I tried to yank away, but whatever had me would not let go. The crowd was all around me. If I whipped too hard, it might start something I was unprepared to deal with. I walked calmly with whatever was leading me. I gritted my teeth and blinked rapidly, fighting guilty tears.

Finally, the voices faded out, and the street was empty. I pulled my arm abruptly into my chest. I had been cooperating, and the move was unexpected. The body of the creature slammed into me. I reared back, ramming my knee into the gut of the creature; it grunted and gasped for air. The hand released me, and I scrambled straight into a wall, and then I crawled on all fours as my captor shuffled after me.

"Lindy!" Came the frantic whisper, "Lindy, stop, you are going to get yourself killed!"

"Onn?" His voice was on the other side of whoever had taken hold of me.

"Listen to the man," a wheezing voice came from the creature. The thing was Daveechi.

"I'm sorry," I said in a voice that conveyed little sympathy. "I didn't know it was you."

"That much was clear," Daveechi said. "Keep quiet now. You will have half the town after us." A hand grabbed my hand, but this time it was Onn, and his grip was safe.

"You're alive!" I whispered. He said nothing in response. But I was sure he squeezed my hand a little tighter. Soon he pulled me into a narrow doorway. It smelled different from his home.

"Daveechi." Onn's voice was hoarse.

"I know all," the Daveechi said. He was angry. "Unfortunately, this complicates our plan."

"What do we need to do?"

"We need to act quickly."

Onn was tense beside me.

"When it is discovered that our own have perished, the people will believe you, Melinda, to be an enemy spy. And it will be challenging to convince them otherwise and to keep you safe, without revealing too much."

"Why not tell them what happened?" Onn said, with his usual startling forthrightness.

Daveechi was silent for a moment. "Matters involving the tyrant are a dangerous business, and my priority will always be to keep our people safe."

It is hard to say whether this answer satisfied Onn, but he did not dispute it.

"I think the best plan of action is to send you with the instrument right away." Daveechi was talking to me now, "You must take it to the canyon and destroy it as planned. This is much earlier than I had planned to send you. I was hoping to help you get better trained." The creature paused. "I am going to send someone with you, a partner, to guide you. Onn." There was a clap as if the creature had brought his hand down on Onn's back. "I am going to send you on this job with Melinda. You did a fine job of getting Melinda safely out of this high-risk situation; yes, I believe you will be right for the job; If you will have it."

A small silence followed this request, but finally, Onn answered, "I'm honored."

"Good! Then you will both leave immediately!" The creature said a little too cheerily.

"Immediately?" Tears were still threatening to brim. "How can we leave? Did you see what happened?" I turned toward Onn, but he said nothing.

"Melinda, as tragic as this is, if you want to avenge your friends, you must carry on the operation," Daveechi said firmly.

I shook my head. "But what about the violin?" I asked, trying to keep my voice from shaking.

"What about it?"

"It is still back with the crowd waiting to be tarred and feathered."

"You say the strangest things, Melinda," Daveechi said under his breath. "Anyway, I have the instrument right here, securely wrapped in a newly woven satchel."

The new satchel dropped over my head and slung around my waist. The material was thicker, more like burlap, and only a little warmth escaped. I twisted my fingers through the strap. *I have to do this.* Deem, Avis, and Magoumi had risked their lives to save me, and I let them die. It was the only way to get rid of the guilt. Besides, there was still the promise of home and Odessa's fortune if I was lucky.

Why was Daveechi sending Onn with me? Onn had admitted he had never been out of the shadow village. Even so, I was glad it was him.

"Here."

Thick material was thrust into my hand. I tucked the cloak between the satchel and my side, and it was like aloe on sun blisters.

"A battlesuit?" Onn's voice questioned. Daveechi must have given him a cloak too.

"It is necessary. Your journey is long."

"One suit takes months to disintegrate," Onn said to me. He was apparently pleased with this fact.

"Did you both eat your fill?" The shadow creature demanded. "You will take food with you, but it will not last more than a few hours above."

"But what will we eat?" I demanded, "And drink? Will drink stay with us?"

"You must return here within three days," the shadow said firmly, "or you will be lost. No one but the tyrant's men can withstand the burning for longer than this."

Onn's footsteps moved toward the supplies, and I turned to follow him.

"Melinda," Daveechi's arms stopped me, "I have not forgotten what I promised you. When you return, I will help you get home. You can count on it."

My jaw stiffened. "Don't you mean *if* I return?"

"Dear girl, let's not think like that," and he let his hand fall to his side with a heavy thump.

CHAPTER 28

D AVEECHI LED US OUT OF the village and to the river. This time the water was cold and refreshing as we waded in. Once again, I saw the gentle ripple of the current and the glint of light buried deep within. The nearly forgotten burning hit my eyes like someone pranking with a mirror, and I twisted away from the glare.

A ferocious splashing signaled that Onn had already dived in. I quickly dove in after him and swam into the remembered lava. Traveling upward toward the light was so much worse than going down. Now the pain only worsened the farther we swam. Every fiber of my being wanted to turn back. *This is the way home. This is the way home.* I repeated to myself. It was like forcing myself to push my hands into a roaring fire. I kept my eyes shut and kept pushing forward—kicking and trying not to slow my pace.

My hand reached out of the water—then the rest of me emerged—choking and sputtering. I wanted to go back to the Shadowlands. It almost wasn't worth trying to get home. I had to move. The light was already piercing through me.

I scrambled onto the rocky ledge of the riverbank and pulled the thick cloak over me—somehow, it was still dry—it brought some comfort. The air was fire to my lungs, but I gasped for it, anyway. I reached down to secure the satchel.

The screaming and panicked splashing had not stopped. Onn was still surfacing. I considered whether I should dive back into the molten stream to help him, but I was rooted to the bank—unable to force myself to dive in.

Onn was swimming frantically toward me. He did not look at all like I had imagined he would. Like the shadow creature, Onn was tall, but this was where the similarities ended. Daveechi was thin and nearly transparent, but Onn was solid. Though his skin was the same shade of charcoal gray, he did not have the pointed figure or sharp edges. Instead, his muscles flexed and were full of life and health. Although his arms still flailed around in the water, swatting at an unknown enemy, his overall demeanor exuded strength and courage.

Perhaps the most peculiar of his features was his hair. It fell about his face and was a striking pale blond—all but white. *Maybe he looks so different from the shadow creature because he's never been exposed to the light. How must I look to him?* Our earlier conversations flickered through my mind.

Onn's cloak was tangled around his neck, and he was so disoriented from the intense pain that he did not fix it. If he was out there much longer, I didn't know what would happen to him. I braced myself, tensing all my muscles, and prepared to wade back into the boiling cauldron of the river.

Before I reached him, a flash of light appeared out of nowhere, and Onn yelped at the sudden pain.

Shining ones.

"Come, come!" the melody called.

I stretched out my hand. "Onn!" He swiftly reached his hand out, and his firm grasp threatened to pull me back under the current. I regained my footing and reached my other hand toward the shore. The shining ones were still calling from the other riverbank. Onn lifted up, as he must have gathered his senses, and we got onto the shore again.

"We must get away from here!" Onn finally spoke, as he was still sputtering to catch his breath, "If they catch us, our operation is over." He passed me and was climbing up ahead.

"Pull your robe over you and get behind here," I shouted, pointing to the rock.

"No time!" He said, already pulling my arm and running, "We cannot let the shining one near us."

The shining ones were gliding through the river toward us. Their voices like the legends of mermaids luring us to our death with their enchanting song.

I began running after Onn, who was flinging his cloak around him as he ran. He took turns with confidence as if he had taken this trek a thousand times. Finally, he dashed behind a rock ledge. I didn't slow down enough and slid across the rock, swinging around its corner, before plopping down beside him. He was attempting to stifle his panting breath as he peered around the corner.

"Gone. We lost them."

"Good." I cleared my throat. The darkness of the village had offered a safety net. I had caught a glimpse of Onn in the Shadowlands, but the confusion hadn't allowed me to *see* him. I was sitting next to a stranger. "Your cloak." I motioned to the dark fabric haphazardly tossed around his shoulders in a tangled mess.

"Would you?" He was not the least bit perturbed by the first sight of me. *He has not seen anything before this day. Why isn't he amazed or at least in shock?* I carefully unwound the robe and hung it protectively around him. He lifted the hood over his head, and the darkness hid him once more. Only his gray eyes and solemn profile were visible now. "We must keep going. Three days will go by fast."

I shook my head. "Only if you're having fun."

Onn glanced back but did not acknowledge my comment.

"How will you know the way?" I said, realizing for the first time no one had given us directions.

"The grid." He closed his eyes and retraced memorized patterns in the air. Before I even had a decent chance to look around, Onn was off again. I glanced around. Onn did say Shadians learned a map of the upper lands much like they learned around the Shadow Village, but I did not expect it to be this effective. He was utterly confident in his direction.

"How far to the canyon?" I stumbled over the sharp rocks lining the shadowed portion of the rock face.

"We must find the path through the woods. The canyon is on the other side of the woods."

"We have three days. Already our water has nearly disappeared."

He took a drink and then handed the bottle to me. I tilted my head back and drank the last swallows. I had already been informed there was no point in trying to save it. It would dry up before the end of the day if we didn't drink it now.

Onn nodded but did not change his stride. "An inn is hidden at the center of the woods. It's a little over halfway to the canyon. We need to make it there tonight, so we can get to the canyon tomorrow and then begin our journey home."

I shook my head. Three days never seemed so short.

CHAPTER 29

"How is it you do not seem at all, I don't know, in awe of everything around you?"

Onn walked with direction and purpose. "It is the tyrant's land. It is to be reviled, not revered."

"Well, I mean, yes, but . . . "

He was looking at me now.

"I mean, you've lived in the Shadow Village all your life. You've always been in darkness. It is the first time you have seen trees, water, rocks, *anything*!"

"It is the first time I have been above, but it is not the first time I have seen."

Those last moments flashed through my mind.

"I wish to unsee what I have seen."

I walked on quietly for a moment. "But this, I mean, this is different. You have to feel something looking at all this!" I waved my hand at the staunch trees, the vibrant blue of the sky against the dark green of their branches. Bright wildflowers lined the path, and the rush of the river still lingered in the distance.

"Yes, I see it. I see it, and it is more painful than the burning on my skin," Onn said with anger mounting in his voice, "All of this! All of this is what the tyrant keeps from my people. We live in the dark while he enjoys it." He glanced down at me. "Even you. This whole time we've been together, your beauty was hidden." He said it as if he were describing the surrounding nature, but it still caught me by surprise.

"The tyrant has robbed everything from us. I have only seen my mother once, and it was in a moment of terror. One cannot notice beauty in fear." He fell silent.

"But surely—"

"Shhhh—" Onn held his hand up. He motioned me to get off the path. I recognized it immediately. It was the same light that had destroyed our friends. There were three of them now—the shining ones—and the light was as powerful as ever.

"They block our path," Onn said.

"Can we take another way?"

"We can't take more time."

Come to the king. They said with the unchanging song, and *He will take the burning away from you.*

"Close your ears to them."

Onn did not seem to hear me. "We do not have time to wait for them to move."

"They won't get too close. If they destroy us, we won't be no use to the tyrant."

"We are no use to him whether we live or die," Onn said in a muffled voice.

I didn't have time to question what he meant by this. In a moment, I set my course of action. With a yell that I hoped was a battle cry, I ran toward the shining ones, stooping to catch up rocks and hurling them as I ran.

"Lindy!"

I did not stop. I was blinded by the pure light all around me. Still, I threw every rock I laid my hand on.

CHAPTER 30

I AWOKE TO FIND MYSELF BEING shoved into a foxhole. Trees surrounded me, and the wind whispered above my head. Onn's eyes were not on me as he attempted to push me into safety while not drawing attention.

"Onn," I said, rubbing my pounding head.

He turned to me quickly. "You live!"

"Did we defeat the shining ones?" I asked, with growing astonishment at my actions.

"They've gone, whatever happened. We will talk more inside."

He firmly motioned to the earthen opening.

I wiggled my way in. It was much like the one the shadow creature had brought me to my first day. "Onn, tell me what happened? Did they get overwhelmed by the rocks?" *Stupid question.* I bit the inside of my cheek.

Onn pulled the branches back over the opening of our underground cave. In the semi-darkness, I did not feel as shy around him. It was more like when we first met.

"Well?" I questioned.

Onn sighed, "I do not understand it." His jaw stiffened. "You should be no more!" He said, "Why would you ever do such a foolish thing? Throwing rocks at them?" All the pain from the last days surfaced in his voice.

"But I am still here."

This infuriated him more. "Yes, and why? All the shining ones would have to do is not move, and you would have dissipated."

"Did they move?"

Onn let his hand drop to his side. "They vanished, as they are apt to do."

"Maybe I hit them with one of my rocks?" I said, not believing it even as I spoke.

"You are a shadow compared to them. Don't you get that? It is like a toddler attacking a lion."

"You talk as if you wanted me destroyed." A knot grew in my chest.

He did not relax. "It does not make sense. Why should they let you live?"

"The violin is of great value. Maybe they need it in one piece."

"They have great power." Onn turned on his side to look at me. My cheeks burned, but this time it was not from the light. "You have seen what they can do," he said.

I bit my lip. "Does anyone ever go with the shining ones?"

"Yes, some," Onn rolled onto his back once again, "but none were seen again." Onn paused, "It was my fault, you know."

"Onn, it was not your fault." I bowed my head, unable to look at him.

"It was my idea to stop the shining ones, "Onn's voice betrayed his battle to fight back the tears. "I just thought, you know, if we stop them from coming into our village. You know, one step forward. I told them we were not ready. I told them—" Onn slammed his fist into the dry dirt wall beside him. The force sent a shower of dust onto both of us and brought horrible flashbacks to my mind.

"Onn, I have to tell you something. You can't blame yourself for this. It—I . . . "

"What do you mean?"

I began to recount to him what had happened and how I had snuck off to another midnight meeting. I told him about how my song had collapsed the secret room and how Avis, Deem, and Magoumi had risked death to save me from being buried alive.

"Your song did all this?" Onn said without emotion.

"Yes, Onn, you have to believe me. I had no idea that would happen. I still don't understand why it happened."

"The music," Onn said, and his voice was tired, "it belongs to the tyrant."

"Onn, I'm so sorry."

"I don't understand why any of this makes you feel that what happened is your fault."

I stared down at the dusty ground beneath me. "Avis, he—well, they all asked me to join them. They saved my life, so I agreed. I promised I would fight with them." I swallowed hard, "But when the time came, I froze. Avis, Deem, Magoumi—they saved my life, risking their own, and when the time came for me to repay the favor, I stood there, and . . . watched them die." I broke away from his gaze and stared hard at the ground.

Onn was silent for a long time.

He must hate me now.

He cleared his throat and said in a whisper, "I'm glad you didn't join them."

I crossed my arms, still avoiding his gaze.

He raised his hand in a broad gesture. "This was the strength of one shining being against three of us, but even with twenty of us, the result would have been the same. We cannot openly attack the tyrant. If you had joined them, there would have been four deaths instead of three, and what good would that have done?"

"Still, I should have told you. You could've stopped it—talked them out of—"

"No," Onn said, tears brimming in his eyes, "Nothing would have stopped them. If I had known, I would not have let them do it without me."

I sat silently for a moment, unsure of what to say.

"The shining one vanished, but it will be back."

I put my hand on his arm, "perhaps your people are stronger than you know."

Onn pulled his arm away from me and turned over. The black cloak rose and fell in the feign of sleep.

I rested my arm over my eyes, wondering how long it would be before I slept in my own bed. Being in this hole in the ground was suffocating. My mind was crowded with memories. Every time I tried to close my eyes, it was happening again. The walls were coming down around me. This time Avis, Magoumi, and Deem were in the pit—being buried alive while I stood above and watched.

CHAPTER 31

"WHAAAAHAAA!" I AWOKE TO FIND my arm stretched out of my cloak and my hand fully exposed to the light. It was the sight of it that made me scream. My hand was thin as paper.

My scream woke Onn, and he calmly placed my robe over the offending hand, the burning eased, and my hand regained solidarity. With my other hand, I reached foolishly into the satchel to make sure the violin remained intact, but the instrument's heat drove my hand away. "Is there any more food?'" I whined, "my stomach feels like it is going to eat itself."

"Our lack of drink should be your greater concern."

"What about the Inn? Do we have time to stop there for food and drink?"

"This is the Inn."

"This?" I rolled my eyes. "Oh c'mon, I've heard of holes in the walls, but really? This is the Inn?"

Onn ignored my displeasure and made his way out.

"I mean, I was not expecting a five-star place, but a complimentary breakfast would have been nice. Or a bed!" Onn was back on the trail now and did not so much as a glance again at me. "Don't forget to turn in your key!" I yelled as I stomped out after him.

We didn't walk much further before we were out of the woods. Neither of us mentioned what had taken place the night before. We simply walked. It was soon time to say farewell to the shade. As we stood at the tree line, it was no mystery where the canyon was located. It would only take us about half a day to reach our destination. I scowled. Onn must have carried me for a long distance. The canyon was narrow, more like a fissure.

"It will be bigger when we approach it," Onn said, marching onward.

This theory did not hold up, however. The closer we came to the canyon, the narrower it appeared. Soon we were standing at the edge of the chasm.

"I can't see the bottom," I said, clutching the satchel.

"That is why it is perfect. The light does not get to the bottom. It is out of the tyrant's reach."

"Why don't your people live here then?"

"The canyon is far from any resources. The journey to get them would be far too dangerous to make regularly. We already risk enough as it is."

"So, what do we do now?"

Onn breezed past me. In one swift movement, he hopped into the crack of the canyon, allowing his legs to enter and bracing his elbows on either side of the rocky edges. His legs were braced against either wall as well.

"You coming?" He asked, squinting up at me.

I grinned at him. "Geronimo!" I dropped in front of him, so there were only about six inches between us.

"Are you completely insane?!" He frantically whispered, "You will bring this whole place down! Not to mention give away our position."

"Onn, I don't think I've ever seen you smile," I said, smirking at him.

"If you keep this up, you never will."

I tilted forward and squinted into the darkness. *Can't see a thing.* "Well, at least I don't have to worry about my fear of heights." My arms, bared to the searing light, were feeling thin. The rest of me, however, was marvelously refreshed.

Onn was feeling the rocky walls with his left toe. At last, he found another foothold, and his left hand disappeared into the dark sanctuary. I followed suit, reaching my foot out and blindly groping for stepping stones. This was going to be a long, tedious trip down. "We should have brought a rope."

"And risk someone seeing it?" I imagined the scoff Onn's face held at this moment. "The shining ones rarely venture this far, but if they found our rope, all they would need to do is burn it through, and we would be shards of flesh on the rocks below."

"Well, at least we would have completed the job," I muttered as I crept another inch downward. "And how do you know that will not be our fate, anyway? I've not exactly been working out."

"Then save your breath, Lindy."

It didn't seem like we had not been climbing down long, yet already we were surrounded by the darkness of the canyon. The canyon's opening was like a lightning bolt permanently etched in a black sky above us. And soon, even this disappeared. This darkness was not comforting darkness like it was in the village. It was empty. The only sound was the scraping of feet being placed carefully on a rock. Yet, the violin was strangely growing stronger despite all of this. It was digging into my side like a fire-poking iron. It was impossible to reposition for fear of falling.

"Onn?"

"Yes?" His voice came from below me.

"Why are we climbing down this pit?"

"What do you mean?" The annoyance rang in his voice, "that is the job."

I was silent for a moment, but I had stopped climbing. "Nooooo," I said, slowly bracing myself with both legs and my left arm still clinging to the wall. "Our job was to destroy the violin."

"Lindy, whatever you are thinking of doing, don't."

His caution came too late. The violin's heat nearly drove my hand back, but I pressed past it, and in one quick grasp, I had it by the neck; I gasped with pain—worried it would burn my hand right off. I hurriedly raised the cursed instrument over my head and flung it into the dark chasm below.

Silence. Onn didn't know what I had done. My heart raced. I held my breath and glanced in Onn's direction. Then it happened.

The first loud clank. It must have hit the canyon wall. The clanking continued, and I pictured the beautiful violin colliding with the canyon walls like a bouncy ball in a hallway.

"Melinda! Did you drop it?"

"No," I said, trying to steady my voice, "I *threw* it."

I waited for Onn to spout off whatever obscenities this world contained, but he didn't say a word, and the only sound was the final crashing of the fiddle's fall.

However, before the violin found its resting place at the bottom of this pit, a *scream* echoed through the crevice walls. Rocks began falling all around us. I had to stop myself from shielding my face. I was afraid I was going to lose my grip. The scream was high-pitched and raspy. And familiar.

A rock came crashing down on my hand. I shrieked and pulled my hand to my chest. More stones were raining down around me. In the next moment, my foot slipped, and I was tumbling down, down. My hands wrapped around my head as I knocked between the walls. The pain was intense, and I wanted nothing more than to become part of the surrounding blackness, but that relief was not to be. A shot of pain raced through my arm, and I let go of my head, screaming. My head squarely hit a rocky ledge, but I remained conscious—wholly conscious of every bruising rock and scrape. I started clawing at the walls, trying to regain a hold.

I kicked my legs out, and my back slammed against the wall. A sharp pain went up to my left leg, but I was still falling; my back was scraping down the rocks. I wasn't screaming anymore. I was gritting my teeth, forcing myself to keep my legs extended and my back against the other side. I had to slow down. Rocks were still falling, and I wanted to cover my face, but I held my hands against the wall behind me, grabbing at the jutting rocks as I scraped past. My body jack-knifed, but my speed was decreasing. Slowing down only made the fall more painful. The jagged wall dug into my back and arms. Then, without warning, I hit the ground with a hard jolt that knocked the breath out of me and sent shockwaves through my whole body.

CHAPTER 32

"Lindy!" Onn's voice was far away.

I slowly reached up and touched my head. It was sticky with blood. I clenched my teeth. *I broke my butt.*

"Lindy! Please don't be dead."

"I'm here."

His voice was far away. "I'm coming," He shouted. "Hold on!"

One pain had vanished. In the deep darkness, nothing burned. Not an ounce of light reached me. The fiddle was destroyed. If it wasn't for the massive amount of pain wracking my body, I might have been relieved. It was over. *Next stop: home.* This knowledge made the pain worth it—almost. I turned my focus back to standing.

I groaned. My head was throbbing. I clutched the rocky wall, and a shock of pain went through my hand. *It's got to be broken.* I tried not to move any more than I had to. The cuts on my arms and back were pulling and tearing even more with each movement. I took another shuffling step forward. My foot hit something, and a *"twang"* resonated off the cavern walls. I shook my head, making my head ache even more, "Dagburnit!" I kicked the thing with what strength I had, and the object, unmistakable now, clattered and twanged across the stone. It was the violin—whole and in one piece. Yet, something was different. In the Shadowlands, the instrument had still exuded light, but now it was invisible in the darkness. I picked it up carefully, feeling every ache as I did so. It was cool to the touch.

"Lindy? Are you moving? Stay where you are."

I tilted my neck and slid the fiddle back into the satchel. "I'm fine," I dragged forward across the rock bottom. "I've always liked a good shortcut."

"Would you just—please, don't move."

"Onn, I think I can climb. Don't come down; let me come to you."

"You're not too hurt?"

"We'll never know unless I try," I said, feeling around for a foothold.

"Does anything else feel broken? Can you bend your arms and legs? "

"In working order."

"That's lucky. We'd never get you out of here with broken limbs."

"My fingers got smashed pretty hard on my right hand." I grimaced as I tried to lift myself. "I don't think I can grip anything with them."

"You will have to either use your forearm or your elbow to climb back out."

I patted my head cautiously and winced at the sticky feeling of hair matted with blood. I used my elbow to lift myself. It took a lot more strength to climb up than down. "The rope idea is not looking so stupid now," I muttered to myself.

I was about three feet from the ground when something brushed my face and rested on my shoulder. I turned staunchly out of habit, not expecting to see anything. My heart dropped. A ghostly figure danced before me.

"No," I stood looking at it, "no, it can't be you." I do not know if I said the words or if they stuck in the back of my throat. I shook my head rapidly, my lips pressed in a tight line.

The *thing* did not move its mouth, but a raspy voice came from it: "take us with you."

I was too scared to scream. I held onto the rock wall, forgetting my pain as I stared at the *thing*. It appeared to float forward. *How can I see it? It was pitch black* down here. The *thing* was not emitting any light. It was like someone had drawn it with a white crayon on a black page.

"Take us with you."

"Are you saying something to me, Lindy?"

I dropped to the ground and started running. There, in front of me, was a minefield of the lightless *things*. They bobbed eerily. The more I stared at them, the more familiar they became. The same voice came again from them. "Take us with you."

I tried to run back, but they were all around, but only one voice. I was having trouble breathing now, and tears were streaming down my face. I began frantically climbing up the rock wall. The pain didn't matter now. Hands pulled at me, trying to pull me down, or maybe they were hoping I would pull them up.

"Take us with you."

With the weight of the things pulling down on me, I was making no progress. I would be stuck here forever.

"Melinda, take us with you."

"No!" I screamed. I desperately tried to kick them off. I was clawing the rock, but they dragged me back down. My nails were scraping across the stone, and it tore at my skin. It knew my name, "Onn!" I screamed, "Help me!" I was about to be pulled into this sea of ghosts. My hands were wrenched from the walls.

"Where are you?" His voice was close.

"I'm here! Right here!" I had completely lost my grip. I reached forward, still touching the cold stone with my fingertips, and kicking at the *things* behind me with what strength I had left.

Then a welcomed hand clasped mine. Onn was pulling me up toward him. Ghostly hands still tore at my legs; it was like cat claws digging into my skin. I reached my other hand, grabbed Onn's forearm, and attempted to scramble up the wall, but it was like I was running in place. Onn's heavy breath was on my face. His arm was tense as he kept his balance while pulling me up out of the monster's grasp. His hand gripped my arm now, and I pulled up and held onto his shoulder so hard my nails dug into his skin. He did not shrink away but continued to pull me higher. The chilling voice was fading.

"Take us with you."

I kept kicking at them, and my feet were still striking them, although less frequently. Onn shifted, and his other hand was holding me. He was bracing himself—a foot on each wall, and now his hands were around my waist. He had a much firmer grip now, and I began kicking at the creatures with greater force, though it didn't make any difference. I was now entirely trusting Onn's strength to keep us both from plummeting down again.

We were face to face now, and I reached above his head for a rocky ledge. Onn pushed me upward. The creatures would be after him next. I reached down for his hand, then all at once, the things let out witchy shrieks that made me jump out of my skin. My own scream caught at the back of my throat. Onn was no longer holding me up. The *thing* was attacking him—pulling him down.

"Go, Lindy—keep climbing!" Onn's voice. They had him, and they were pulling him down with them. My eyes were wide with terror. The dreadful *things* were clamoring around what must be Onn. "Take us with you." The raspy voice continued to crone.

Not again. I began scrambling downward. Down toward the nightmare of all nightmares. "Onn!" I barely managed to find my voice. There was no answer. I was getting closer to the *thing*, and I wasn't even breathing. I had to get to Onn. "I can't see you. I can't see you," I screamed. The *thing* was moving too fast; I would never catch up to it. I stopped climbing and covered my face. I was sobbing now. The ripping at my leg began again. I didn't struggle against the pull anymore, and I was being carried back down into the dark chasm.

"Lindy." It had to be Onn, but his voice had never been like this before.

I couldn't speak.

"Sing!" the tortured voice managed to get the word out.

Sing. I opened my mouth, but nothing came out. I began struggling against the hellish hands again, reaching upward and using all my strength. *Sing*. I still wasn't breathing. I opened my mouth, but the song was stuck deep in my throat. *Onn. Sing*!

I shouted the words:

I'm pressing on the upward way,

New heights I'm gaining ev'ry day[2]

No earthquake, and the *things* were unphased. "Take us with you." Onn was no longer screaming.

I panted, still kicking against the *things* but making no progress as more and more of them swarmed me. *Sing*!

I forced a deep breath, then I bellowed the screechiest, worst-sounding song ever imagined. My voice broke with every note, but I sang:

I want to scale the utmost height,

And catch a gleam of glory bright;

But still I'll pray till heav'n I've found,

"Lord, lead me on to higher ground."[3]

The *things* started shrieking like an army of bats startled out of slumber, and they immediately released me and started fleeing downward. I stopped singing and focused my energy on holding on to the walls as rocks and debris fell all around me. *Onn*. "Onn!"

Silence.

"Onn!"

A quiet scraping sound was making its way up the wall. It slowly inched its way closer to me. I took a slow breath as I peered into the darkness below. "Onn?" I said with a shaky voice. An arm wrapped around my waist, whether it was to steady himself or to steady me, I didn't know. I didn't care. Onn was alive. I kept glancing down, expecting to see the lightless *things* chasing us, but they had disappeared below. We started climbing again. I was shaking with the incredible fear of the living hell that threatened to catch up to us. The darkness made it feel like we were making no progress, and the constant fear hung over us that at any moment, we might hear that voice again. The pain returned. I was aware of every ache, open wound, and sprain each time I moved. The air here was cold

2. Johnson Oatman, Jr.. *Higher Ground*. hymnary.org

3. Johnson Oatman, Jr.. *Higher Ground*. hymnary.org

and stale. Burning was better than this. *The fiddle.* After all that, I still had it. It was icy by my side now.

Onn's sole created a steady rasp as he climbed beside me, but my mind imagined the sound was the ghost beings clawing their way up after us. Pain shot through my crushed fingers up to my elbow. In some ways, the pain was comforting. Without it, I was sure we were climbing up a downward escalator into insanity.

Finally, the opening of the canyon yawned above us. This time the light brought something I did not expect: hope.

Onn was above me. I turned my focus back to my climbing. *Keep going.* Then, Onn extended his hand down to mine. He had reached the surface. Relief washed over me. I took his hand and clamored out of the scar that marred this world. We sat there. In the full and unabashed light—our legs still dangling over the edge—both of us gasping for air. Onn did not take his eyes off me.

We were in some sort of trance. Both of us were locked in a sadness we didn't understand. I might have convinced myself that none of it happened—that I hit my head too hard on the way down. However, my legs were covered in blood. Claw marks ran up and down, and my pants were shredded up to the mid-thigh on my left leg. I bit my lip, trying to stop the tears. Onn said nothing, but he pulled me over to him, and I leaned on his shoulder.

"We must find shelter." It was Onn who finally broke the silence. We were both growing thin from the light. Neither of us wanted to say what was on our minds. It would be impossible to get to even the Inn before the three days were up. We had completed our assignment, but it was not the violin that was destroyed at the bottom of the canyon.

CHAPTER 33

"WHERE ARE WE?"

"We're hiding in a bush," came Onn's even reply, "You are too weak to travel."

"I'm fine." This was a lie. My injuries, combined with the constant light, had drained my strength.

"Get some rest."

"What was down there?" I asked, ignoring his remark.

"I don't know."

"Did you see them?" My whole body was tense.

"Yes." His voice remained even.

"Then, you know. You do!" I wanted to punch him.

"It was in our minds. Just in our minds."

"In our minds?" I was shaking now. "Magoumi, Avis—" My voice broke, "those were your friends. Your friends. And then so many others—" I pounded my fist into the ground. "What else is in our minds? Is what they did to us in our minds?" I waved my leg in Onn's solemn face. "All of them. The tyrant does not make them vanish. He puts them *there*. Where they become those *things*!" I was on the verge of sobbing now. "Deem and Avis, and all the—"

"Stop!" Onn stood and paced. "It was not them."

"Do you think we both had the same hallucination?"

"By all that's dark, do you ever stop talking?" Onn threw his hands in the air and let them rest on the back of his head.

"Don't you act like you're the only one who has lost something here." I was yelling now—adrenaline still coursing through my veins. "I know what the situation is. We have no more food. I can't travel quickly—" my voice broke, "I'm never going to see anyone I love again. I'm—I'm going to die in this unknown world far away from my family. And, and . . . they'll never know what happened to me."

Onn closed his eyes and sat down in the grass. "Just let me think."

I shook my head angrily and brushed away tears. "Fine. What are we going to do now?"

"I told you, get some rest," Onn said through his teeth.

"I mean for 'the cause.' What are we going to do with the fiddle?"

Onn stopped short and stared at me. When he spoke, his voice was rigid. "What do you mean? It is gone—broken in a thousand pieces at the bottom of the canyon. Tell me this is so."

"No," I said and pulled open my satchel. "It is right here."

Onn reached out as if to take it, but I held it out of his reach. He pulled back and put his head in his hands. "Lindy! You threw it. It is gone!"

I sat silently. The instrument in my hand was still cool to the touch and undamaged from its plunge into the abyss. I ran my broken fingers over the chilled surface. My thumb ran across a small chip in the smooth wood: such a fall and only a tiny blemish.

"Onn."

He did not raise his head.

"Onn, I have been on the wrong job." I shook my head and hurried on before he interrupted me. "I would not even be here if not for Mrs. Aidan Odessa." Trying to remember Mrs. Odessa was like trying to recall a forgotten dream. I reached my hand into my pocket. The small piece of paper was still there. The instructions were spelled out in the same handwriting. I didn't know how I had held onto it through everything.

"We are going to the waterfall."

"Are you insane? Why in all that is dark would we ever think of—"

I lifted the violin towards him.

Onn stared at me for a full minute. "Why do you still have it?" He said in a whisper.

"I—"

"It is supposed to be lost forever in a thousand pieces. That was the job. The only job."

"Onn, it didn't break. It is completely whole except—"

"Can you do anything right?" Onn's face darkened. "All you had to do was follow orders! Take the instrument to the bottom of the canyon and destroy it. But no. No, you had to *throw* it. Even after that, you find it again in one piece, but instead of destroying it, you bring it back with you as a souvenir."

"I understand why you are upset, but—"

"Oh, do you, Lindy?"

"Listen to me!"

"I'm done listening. Because of your foolishness, we have destroyed nothing but ourselves." Onn turned his back to me and limped into the woods.

I let go of the violin and jumped to my feet. I was already stiff, and the gaping wounds all over me pulled and tore as I stood, but the rage was boiling inside of me and was taking over. "Onn!" He did not turn. "Onn! Don't you walk away from this!" I was screaming now, "you're right. I didn't follow directions or stick to the plan or anything else, but I am now. I wouldn't be here, wherever I am, if I had followed this piece of paper. So that's what I am doing now! We only have a little time until we fry in this weird world, and we need to do what's right. After all that has happened, don't you see we've been doing this all wrong? I'm never going to see my family again; that's a fact. So now I am going to put this blasted violin behind the waterfall because a two-hundred-year-old lady told me to, and I should think if you live to be that old, you should know what you're talking about!"

Onn's pace did not slow.

I started running after him, and not thinking only doing, I jumped on his back, wrapping my arms around his neck and screaming like a wild banshee—partially out of anger and partially out of pain.

Onn began spinning in circles, swatting at me. "What are you doing? Do you wish to bring every shining one in the country down on us?"

"If you care anything at all for your country, you will come with me."

Onn abruptly sat down. He plopped me on the ground behind him with my arms in a crazed chokehold around his neck.

"What is wrong with you?"

"This is our only chance. What do we possibly have to lose?"

He pulled my arms off his neck. "Something is not right about all this."

"Fine." I pushed myself to my feet. "I am going to the waterfall with or without you." I turned my back on him and limped back to the fiddle, awkwardly scooping it up and trying not to groan at the pain all my recent movement had afforded my wounds. I pulled my hood back from my eyes and scanned the horizon. The tattered cloak didn't offer relief. I was bruising and cut all over, and blood was matting my hair. *I need to get to the water and wash these wounds, although I'm not sure what the point is if I'm going to die of starvation. The river is where I need to look for the waterfall. I haven't seen a waterfall this whole time.* I bit my lip. *Don't freak out, Melinda, and don't look at him.*

"You're terrible at bluffing; you know that, right?" Onn was standing right beside me.

"I don't know what you're talking about," I said, sticking my nose in the air and limping, trying to appear confident, forward with the fiddle securely in my grasp.

"It's this way."

I turned to see Onn walking in his steady stride to the east. He didn't seem to have sustained as many injuries as me.

I limped after him. *Ha! Terrible at bluffing, he says. I played you like a fiddle.*

Onn stalked on silently ahead.

We trudged up the riverbank. Neither of us was taking the precautions we had taken thus far. We walked right in the open, hardly caring about our exposure, though we still wrapped what was left of our cloaks tightly around us. If we made it to the waterfall and the tyrant captured us, at best, we would be like leaves in a fire, and at worst, we would become the shadows of shadows lost forever in the pit. I shuttered, thinking of it. Even if we returned the violin and made it out unharmed by some miracle, we would never make it back to the Shadow Village.

It had been two days since we had any food or drink. My hair was sticky as the sweat mingled with old blood. My hand had already turned a deep shade of purple, and my legs still had open sores, most of which probably required stitches. Onn was visibly slowing his pace to allow me to keep up with him. Every step was painful. It was a constant reminder of the fate that likely awaited us and the pain that would not relent.

We reached the river, and I stopped and tried to wash the blood from my head and skin and clean out the cuts in my legs and back. It was like trying to bathe in boiling water, but I washed everything clean, and it brought a little relief.

"Here, let me have your satchel," Onn said. I handed it to him, and he tore it into cloth strips. He then wound the makeshift bandages around my legs and over the gash on my head. The jagged slashes in my back were a hopeless cause. "There, it might not help much, but it will keep the dust out of the sores," he said, stepping back to assess his work. Onn was also covered in cuts and scratches, but his were not as deep as mine. Many of my injuries were incurred with the first fall I took.

I smiled weakly. "It feels better. Cleaner." I was growing tired and struggled to get to my feet. Onn's brow wrinkled. "We better get going," I said, trying to act more robust than I was. Onn reached his hand around my waist and pulled my arm around his shoulder, supporting me as we walked.

CHAPTER 34

T HIRST MADE MY THROAT LIKE sandpaper and the air like sawdust. The river taunted us. I was beginning to think it might be worth it to taste lava.

"Tell me why the violin matters so much," my voice was like gravel.

Onn was bearing most of my weight at this point. "Tell you? You already know. You learn all about it in the Shadowlands."

"I know, I know, but—" I swallowed hard, trying to moisten my parched throat. "I need you to tell me. Talk to me, Onn. I can't focus on this pain."

Onn glanced down at me with a worried expression on his face. Still, he cleared his throat and began in storytelling fashion to rehash the story of the fiddle, "Legend says, the tyrant will only allow unblemished perfection in his courts." Onn was panting. "He gathers the best of the best. The best musicians play the best instruments for his pleasure."

I nodded slowly, still focusing on plodding forward.

"Odessa stole the violin. Now his collection is incomplete." Onn glanced back at me. "Imperfect."

"Wait," I said, scrunching my eyebrows together, "Daveechi send us to get on the tyrant's nerves?"

"Without the instrument, things are not the way the tyrant made them be, which makes it closer to what Daveechi wishes to make it."

I drew in a long, raspy breath.

"Don't you see? Imperfection is why everything is the way it is," Onn said.

"I don't think I understand."

Onn sighed, "Since the first rebellion, the tyrant has regarded us as imperfect. The tyrant destroys what does not live up to his standards."

"How can he—"

"So Daveechi's plan is to take something that is the tyrant's own—this instrument here—and destroy its perfection. Then the tyrant can no longer claim that his kingdom is without fault. Daveechi hopes this will cause the tyrant's entire kingdom to implode."

I ran my thumb over the chip in the violin's smooth surface, "How can destroying an instrument do anything at all, much less end the tyrant's reign?"

"That is what Daveechi was *hoping*. He has no proof that it would be effective, but surely it would accomplish something."

"The tyrant is a monster," I said in disbelief.

"Yes, unless—"

"Unless what?"

"Do you . . . " Onn shook his head and peered into the distance, " . . . do you claim to be perfect, Lindy?" He asked in an even tone.

"Of course not; no one can."

"The tyrant does."

"The *tyrant* claims to be perfect?" The words burst out without any consideration, "Anyone can look around and see that is not remotely true."

"Still, if it was true, who can stand before perfection?" Onn had a far-off look in his eyes as if he was actually considering if the tyrant's actions were justified.

I winced as the throbbing in my head increased, and I turned to face forward once more. "What's going on with you, anyway?" I asked as I used my free hand to massage my temple.

Onn scowled. "What are you talking about?"

"You're not acting like yourself."

"Well, for starters, I have had nothing to eat or drink for the past two-and-a-half days, and I am following a madwoman to the one place that will lead to certain death. But, hey, please excuse my lack of enthusiasm for small talk. How are you doing?" Onn sighed, and the look on his face showed he immediately regretted lashing out. "Lindy, I'm sorry, you're hurt—"

I smiled and didn't even mind the cracking of my parched lips. I pulled my arm down from around Onn's neck, and I reached out and grabbed his hand. It was a different hand than the first time I held it. Now this hand had callouses, bruises, and scrapes that bore witness to all we had been through together. "I'm glad you are following." I lifted my head, peering straight into his gray eyes, and I almost forgot the light blazing on my face. "I wouldn't have made it this far without you."

Onn's gaze softened, and he tightened his grip on my hand.

"Ow! ee! Careful there, that's the bruised one."

"I'm so sorry," Onn said, immediately releasing my hand. I reached over and took it back again. And so, we walked hand in hand in silent solidarity like we used to back in the Shadowland. My tongue stuck to the roof of my mouth, and I was getting light-headed. Onn pushed us to move faster, but neither of us managed more than a steady plodding. The memories that haunted my mind were too heavy to bear. We put one foot in front of the other, not speaking or thinking. I raised my head for a moment and caught a glimpse of large boulders ahead of us, which promised some relief from the light.

"Children!" a voice said from behind the first boulder. "I have been worried sick about you two!" Daveechi crept out, remaining hidden from the light.

Onn dropped my hand. He stood rigidly, and his face was full of distrust.

Daveechi was tucked between a large boulder and a bush by the river and beckoned us to him. I turned toward him, but Onn stared ahead and continued his faltering pace. I adjusted my satchel strap and followed suit, although I did not understand why.

Daveechi, seeing we were not coming to him, slunk out of the safety of the shadows and crept carefully beside us, "Onn, Melinda! Why do you not greet me? I have brought you supplies. I grew worried when there was no sign of you."

"Save it, Daveechi. We will take nothing from you."

"Nothing?" I whispered to Onn, "If he has food—"

Onn raised his hand to signal me to stop talking.

"My boy, you would refuse food and drink from my hand? I, who have been like a second father to you these many years?"

"I will take nothing from you," Onn repeated.

"You will die for stubbornness?" Daveechi whined, "come back home with me, child. I will help you get home safely."

Onn stopped walking and turned to face Daveechi. "What is it you want? You clearly can't take us back after everything we've seen. Why stop us now if we are going to die? Wouldn't that be the easiest way out for you?"

"Onn, what are you talking about?" I pulled him, so he was facing me.

"Lindy, don't you see that this whole thing has been a suicide mission? And *he* planned it from the beginning."

"Onn, I would never—"

"If we had followed his directions to the letter, we would have both been at the bottom of the canyon with those monsters, and we would never escape."

"If you didn't know, how would he know?" My head was spinning from the heat.

"He knows a lot more than he lets on, right Daveechi? My real question is, why? Why do it? Why keep all the people from knowing the truth. We have not waged a single battle against the tyrant, and you want to keep it that way. You sent us, the only two who witnessed Magoumi, Deem, and Avis's attack, to die at the bottom of the canyon, and now you are here trying to keep us from going to the tyrant." Onn was short of breath from this speech, but he continued to walk away from Daveechi.

Daveechi quickly pulled in front of him. "That is quite the theory, Onn, but why all this sudden distrust? You know what the tyrant is capable of."

"No, Daveechi," Onn said, panting and struggling to get the words out for lack of strength, "I know what *you* are capable of, and I intend to find out for myself what the tyrant is capable of."

Daveechi's face hardened. "Fine," he hissed, "I tried to save you; let that be known. You will seal your fate and join the mist." With one swift motion, Daveechi whisked away our black cloaks—our only shield from the light—and was gone.

Before I had even a chance to react, Onn pulled me into the shade of a boulder. I was growing thin even here.

"He knew!" I gasped for breath, "Did you hear? He knew. He knew what he was sending us to in the canyon." I leaned back against the rock, wiping my forehead, even though we were far too dehydrated for there to be any sweat to wipe away. I shook my head, "How did *you* know he knew?"

"I have known Daveechi all my life." Onn's sentences were short and between breaths. "He manipulates. He speaks in riddles. And twists the truth. I convinced myself he had good intentions. But after seeing him turn on even me—"

"So, what is truth?"

"Maybe there is none," Onn attempted to stand but swayed like he was about to faint. I struggled over to him. Without the robe shielding him from the light, he quickly lost strength. I pulled his arm around my shoulder and tried to support him with what little might I had left. I wished Onn would have waited to confront Daveechi until after taking some food and water.

"We are going to our death," Onn said. "I can see no other outcome. Lindy, I'm sorry I convinced you to join me in this."

"Don't talk. We have to save our energy. Come on, all that is left is to go forward."

CHAPTER 35

*T*HIS MUST BE WHAT IT *is like to be lost in the desert.* Thirst. Sweat. Weak. Burnt. Yet, a beautiful mirage surrounded me. Flowers grew along the path. The water rushed beside us. Its cheerful current sounded temptingly crisp and refreshing. The water soon became a deafening roar as we approached what must be the waterfall. The light grew harsher, and I kept my eyes on the ground in front of me to not look at the light. No shining ones had disrupted our path. If one would appear, we would never have the strength to run or hide from it, much less attempt to battle.

I focused all my energy on putting one foot in front of the other. I was no longer even thirsty. My insides were drying out. The roar of the waterfall grew louder and louder, and the blaze of light that must have been coming from it sapped what energy I had left. I slogged forward so slowly it was a wonder I wasn't going backward. Onn wasn't pushing us now. He was thin, nearly transparent, and ashen. *Did I look the same?* He stopped in front of me. I bumped into him, but we both had been moving so slow that I barely made any impact. We were standing in front of an enormous cliff. I had been staring at the ground for so long; I didn't realize we were approaching it. A cascade of light fell like water from the top of the cliff. This must be the waterfall.

"Well," Onn squinted at me, "what is our plan?"

I winced in pain as I gripped the rocky ledge, "Our plan is to keep going."

"Lindy," Onn's cheeks were sunken in. "we don't have the strength to climb to the top of this cliff, especially not out in the light."

I refused to look up to see how high this cliff was. Already, as I pulled myself up to the first foothold, every muscle and injury screamed at me to stop.

Onn was still on the ground. "We'll never make it."

I sighed, looking for the next ledge. "Then we will climb as high as we can until our strength gives out."

Onn shuffled below me and then reached up, grasping a jutting edge. A vision of the *things* flashed through my mind as I pushed myself upward. I held tight to the rocky ledge and clenched my eyes shut for a moment. The light from the falls struck me like someone pouring rubbing alcohol into the deep cuts on my back. I had to take a deep, concentrated breath with each movement to make myself move forward. We were so close to the waterfall's roar, and I kept thinking that if I didn't fall to my death from exhaustion, then the waterfall of fire would burn me into nothing. With each attempt to find another foothold, flashbacks from the day before tormented me. If those *things* belonged to the comfort of pure darkness, then what other terrors did the blaze of pure light hold?

We were moving up the wall like a pair of sloths—arms and legs slowly jutting forward, making painfully slow progress. The violin thumped beside me. Since the instrument was cold, I tied part of the satchel, what was left of it, around the instrument's neck, and it hung around my waist. It had fallen so far and survived, but it had lost more than the chip in its perfect curve. Every part of me ached, except where the violin rested. It now offered cool relief.

Can't hold on much longer. I glanced down. We had made it to a dizzying height. The light grew stronger the higher we climbed. I didn't dare look up to see how much farther we had to go. I didn't look over at Onn either, but his panting indicated he was right beside me, if not above me. Each blink lasted a little longer, and my grip got a little lighter. Very soon, I might faint or even fall asleep from pure exhaustion, but just as my head tilted backward, Onn called, "Lindy, we made it."

I lifted my head ever so slightly. One of his hands gripped the final ledge. I let out a long breath, and then, with every ounce of strength I had left, I pulled myself upward. If I hadn't been in so much pain, it might have been comical how long it took me to do the simple movement. Onn hoisted himself slowly over the edge, and then, lying on his belly at the top, he reached down and pulled me the rest of the way up. I rolled over the edge and laid on my back with my arms thrown across my face. Onn didn't move but lay on his stomach with his arms and head still peering over the edge.

We made it. I pushed myself into a crawling position. "We need to keep moving. This place has to be swarming with shining ones."

Onn stirred, but he held back. In his face was fear. The fear was not fear for himself or his people, but it was a fear that we *ought* not to be here. He had the look of the twelve-year-old with his hand in his grandfather's wine cabinet or of a child caught in a lie at church.

Anger welled up in me. "Go on then," I said, pulling Onn's arm. "Think of all who have perished," I said through my teeth.

He did not move.

What's the matter with him? "Are you okay?"

"I don't know. Maybe this is a bad idea."

"You're waiting until now to decide this is a dangerous plan?" I said a little too loudly. He was standing up now.

"I didn't think we'd make it this far," Onn shrugged and rubbed his arm.

"Well, I didn't come this far to give up now." I turned my back on him in a faltering motion and moved forward. Raising a lone finger in the air, I shouted, "For Odessa!" And with every last ounce of strength in me, I lunged forward toward the waterfall.

The force of the waterfall nearly knocked me back over the cliff. Before I even got close to the rush, the blinding energy of the light hit me. The violin was like ice. With no hood to protect me,

I reached for the fiddle and put it over my face and chest to shield myself from the light. I might have had the strength to press on when I first arrived in this world, but now I had nothing left. I was fading, and I couldn't move or stop it from happening.

Then there was pressure on my ankle. Onn was pulling me back to safety. My determination kicked in, and I jerked away. I was going to succeed or die trying. I scanned the area for a hiding place—any shaded area would do. Onn pulled at me again, this time with more force. In front of me, a dark shadow rushed towards me. It was only then I became aware I was lying on the ground, stomach in the dirt, being dragged backward, away from the falls, away from the light, and away from the pain that threatened to erase me.

The light lessened, only in the slightest. Onn had dragged me under a rock ledge, yet there did not seem to be any shade even here.

"Why did you do that?" I demanded, turning to face Onn.

Only it wasn't Onn.

"This reminds me of how we first met." Daveechi sat, smiling at me. "You really need to learn to avoid these types of situations."

"What do *you* want?" I spat.

"To help you," another voice answered.

I spun around to see the speaker, and there sat Jay, looking smugly at me. "I don't need your help," I said.

Jay turned over his hand, examining his fingernails. "Really? Because the blood and bruises suggest you do."

"Has Onn turned you against me, too? You know as well as I that if it weren't for me, there would be no you," Daveechi said softly.

I pursed my lips and stared at him, edging the violin behind me. "And if it wasn't for him," I said, nodding at Jay, "I might not be here to begin with."

"As I recall, I tried to stop you," Jay said.

"And now we are here to help you get home."

Home. I had completely given up on the idea of ever seeing my home or my family again. "You'll take me home?"

"We will," Daveechi said. "It was what I should have done from the beginning. I'm so sorry for everything you've endured. That's why I've brought Jay. He is going back to Soli, and he can guide you."

"When we get back, I'll even tell Odessa myself that you successfully completed the job," Jay said. "That way, you can still get the reward money for all your trouble."

I bit my lip. It was too good to be true.

"Here. Quick, I almost forgot," Daveechi pulled out another black robe.

Seeing the robe caused resentment to rise again. "Why should you give back what you took?" I asked with disgust.

"What you had was in tatters. I was only trying to—"

"You left us to die!"

"I was only trying to help, and you wouldn't accept it."

I jerked the robe from Daveechi's hand. It brought sweet relief as soon as I put it on, "Where is Onn?"

"Yes, Onn. I'm afraid we have bad news."

I froze. My eyes stay fixed on Daveechi's face.

"Well, you see, I wanted to save both of you, but there was so little time, and Onn, he—he refused my hand . . . "

"What are you saying?" I grabbed hold of the shadow creature's shoulders. His bones were pointed and jabbed into my bruised hands. I shook him and shouted at him, "What are you saying?"

"Melinda. Onn—he is no more." The shadow creature's eyes did not leave my face.

I dropped to my knees, my hands still clutching Daveechi's robe. Pain shot through my arms. I gripped harder.

"There, there, he would want you to be strong—"

"Don't touch me, you snake!" I released his robe and pulled away. "It was you! You wanted us dead!"

Daveechi shook his head kindly, "Child, if I had wanted you dead, why would I have saved you two times?"

I tried to swallow back the tears, but I was too weak, and sobs shook my frame. *No. It can't be right. No. No. No.*

"Uh, I don't mean to pressure you, but we do not have much time," Jay said. "We don't want to risk being seen."

I glared at him and ran my hand through my hair, depositing tears and snot into it. Finally, I stood up. "I have no one now." Every ounce of determination I had was gone.

"You know that I only want what is best for this country and my people."

"What do we do now?"

"Well, if you want to return the violin—"

"I will do anything to avenge Onn and rid the land of this tyrant. I hate the tyrant." I wiped away a stray tear. "I hate everything that is his."

The shadow creature smiled. "As you should. Then we must leave this place, and quickly."

My breath faltered. "Lead the way."

We crept out from the ledge, and to my surprise, we walked further into the light. I wrapped the cloak tightly around me, so there was only a tiny slit for one eye to see out. Since Daveechi had given me a new cloak, my strength returned, although my body was still in pain. "Where are we going? Aren't we leaving the waterfall?"

"Don't you want to destroy the tyrant?"

I scowled deeply. "What about the fiddle?"

"Keep it close." The shadow creature rushed forward. "We are going to present it to the tyrant himself."

CHAPTER 36

D AVEECHI STRODE IN FRONT OF me, checking around corners, and Jay crept behind me. The three of us stayed near the rock ledges, even though they offered no shade. I followed behind numbly. I should have had renewed hope at the prospect of actually returning home, but my mind was empty. Onn was gone. Was he one of the chalky, nameless *things*? A tear escaped. A second slid after it. I was glad the black cloak hid my face from Daveechi and Jay. He contained himself well—too well. He didn't seem bothered at all that Onn, who he claimed to love as a son, had perished. *Daveechi is focused on the job, as you should be too.* I wasn't. I followed the shadow creature blindly. I had lost all care for the violin, the job, and the reward. Even the promise of home only brought more numbness. My thirst to avenge Onn kept me moving forward. I held the violin tightly.

Daveechi halted. He put his arm out to keep me from passing, and I walked robotically into him. A shining one stood in front of us. It carried a shadowy blanket made of the same material as the cloaks. The shadow was huge, taller than Daveechi, and it was coming toward us rapidly.

"Run!" Jay shouted, and I rushed after him and Daveechi but tripped over a leg and fell to the ground. The blanket blocked out the light of the shining one as it loomed over me. I pushed backward frantically. My hood had fallen from my head, and the rest was all draping on my right side, leaving most of me exposed. I was growing weaker every second.

"Daveechi!" No answer.

I was using all of my energy to escape the shining one. I would have to get myself out of this alone. As the shining one drew closer, it became clear it meant to capture me. It held the shadow over me like a net. Then it was here. It stood over me and lowered a dark cloth over me. It was speaking to me, but I did not stop to hear. I started swinging the violin at it with all the fury and grief I had amassed since being in Chaira.

This was the closest I had ever been to a shining one. The dark cloth allowed it to get this close without vaporizing me. Although I was swinging and shouting wildly, it was not scared off as the other shining ones had been with the rocks. I hurled the violin with all the strength I had left, right at its hideously gorgeous face. The violin did not even hit the shining one. Instead, it faded to a mist and disappeared as the shadowy tarp dropped over me. *It is finished. I failed.*

Would they take me to the tyrant? What did it matter, anyway? The fiddle was gone, and soon I would be too.

CHAPTER 37

THE DARKNESS OF MY PRISON brought some comfort. It was enough privacy for me to let my guard down. Now the tears fell unabated. Low wails escaped my lips. I cried for everything I had lost. I cried for a home I would never see again. I cried for Aidan Odessa. I cried for this world. I cried for my own, but more than anything else, I cried for Onn. My tears for him were angry. *Why did he let this happen? He knew the dangers more than anyone. He should still be here.*

It hurt too much to be angry at Onn. *Daveechi!* Onn had been right. Daveechi spoke nothing but lies. He had promised never to leave me, and where was he now? Onn is dead, and now Daveechi would let me die. "He's a liar," I muttered. *I doubt he was ever interested in overpowering the tyrant. He was only ever interested in creating his own kingdom. He used Onn, and he used me.* I'm not sure how long I sat trapped under the cloth, but my strength was returning. The darkness allowed me to grow more solid, and my head stopped throbbing.

"Why have you come?" a loud voice spoke.

When I answered, my voice was childish, though I tried to sound firm, "I wish to see the tyrant."

"To see the king would mean your demise."

I pursed my lips. "Are you a shining one? Will I become a robot like you if I stand before him?"

"You will become mist if you stand before the king as you are now."

My hand instinctively slipped to where the violin used to hang. "Then, I will send your tyrant a message."

"The king welcomes this."

"Tell your *tyrant* I despise him. Tell him anything he is I want never to be." I clenched my teeth. "I would choose to live forever in darkness rather than join him if that is what it took. All I feel toward him is hate, and I will never join his side."

"You speak, but you do not understand," the shining one said.

"I'm telling you what I know."

"Do you presume to be all-knowing?"

This prodding angered me more. "Knowledge comes *from* experience," I said, trying to sound confident, but the fear that had been on Onn's face was now creeping onto my own.

"And what have you experienced?" The voice asked.

"Nothing but pain at your 'king's' hands."

"Tell me of your pain."

I grit my teeth. "He took everything that should be beautiful and made the people of this land live in darkness as their only comfort, and if they dare step into his world and look for happiness there, your tyrant destroys them." Both my hands balled into fists, "He created a world where to see is to burn."

"What you say is true. You are only trusting what you see. But, when you live in the dark, how can you see?"

"Take me to the tyrant."

"It is not time."

"Time?"

"Yes, everything has an appointed time."

I sensed I was alone again. I wanted to go home more than I had this entire trip. I tried to stay awake by nursing my anger, but soon I fell into a restless sleep. I did not dream, but I am sure I cried, even in my sleep.

CHAPTER 38

"L INDY?"

I jerked awake, "Onn?" *Was it Onn? No. He is dead.* I was sitting upright now—listening.

"Lindy, I have so much to tell you."

No, this was not Onn. The voice was like Onn's, but it was the voice of a shining one.

"Who are you?" I could have sworn it was the same smile I had always heard in his voice.

"It's me, Onn."

"I don't believe you." *A hallucination. Makes sense. I've been here for days.*

"Lindy," the voice was warm, "It *is* me."

"If it is you," I shook my head, "what happened to you? You're dead." I was slipping.

"The king."

"The tyrant? Did he take you? Were you forced to join the ranks?"

A laugh came from the shining one. *A laugh. This definitely isn't Onn.*

"Lindy, no one is forced to join the king. The choice is yours. To join the king and have the burning taken away, or to be no more."

"That doesn't sound like much of a choice."

"It is as a child chooses to join a birthday celebration or to go outside and pout."

"It's not you." Tears brimmed in my eyes again. It was another trick—another one of Daveechi's schemes.

He continued, "Everything was a lie. The king is good—"

"Onn would *never* say the tyrant was good. Not after what we have seen."

"Lindy, don't you understand? Please, think about it. If the king wished to destroy us, all he would have to do is speak, and we would be no more. Yet here we remain. My people have lived for centuries after the rebellion."

I grit my teeth, "If it is you, how did this happen to you? Why are you so different?"

"I surrendered to the king."

"No!" I kicked the tarp violently.

"Lindy, yes. It was the best decision I have ever made."

I drew in a slow breath. "And now?"

"And now I am here hoping you will do the same."

"I asked to see the king, and they forbid me to go."

"The time is now. Throw off these shadows."

"You are no better than Daveechi."

"Lindy, trust me. Please, step into the light. It is the only way to know what is true."

I scrunched my eyebrows. "I can't. I'm trapped under here." Light peaked in from between the blanket and the ground. My fists were wrapped around it, and I was holding it to my chest like a security blanket. I wasn't imprisoned; I was in hiding. All I had to do was let go and walk out.

I held my breath as if I were about to dive into the deep end for the first time, and I crept out. There was Onn, or at least a shining one who resembled Onn. He stood a way off, but I still wrapped my cloak around me to block out the pain of the light that poured from him.

I cautiously peered back up at his face. It was the sharpest pain thus far, but his face, I had to see his face. His eyes and mouth held the smile I had heard in his voice so many times but had never seen. It was as if I were looking at Onn as he was meant to be, but as he had never been before. I had to turn away.

"Come and see." He reached out his hand, but I did not take it. Instead, I trailed at some distance behind this so-called-Onn. We walked down a wide hallway, but one side was stone—firm and unmoving—and the other wall bounced and stirred brightly.

"The waterfall. We are behind the waterfall," I muttered to myself.

The music was being played all around me. Shining ones with instruments of every kind blending in an orchestra as beautiful as the light itself. One sound rose above all the rest. It was a violin. *The violin.* It was made new and reunited with its bow at last. A shining one was playing it as it was always meant to be played. The fiddle's song danced off the walls and echoed through the water. It was more beautiful than I had ever imagined.

"How is it possible? It vanished!" I asked, looking around for any signs of an earthquake, but the air remained peaceful.

"With the king, nothing is impossible. After all, it was made for Him!"

"The violin?"

The pseudo-Onn waved a shining arm through the air. "The music!" And as he did, a symphony erupted through the halls, and shining ones fell in around the lone violin player as if in celebration of the instrument's return.

Onn beckoned me forward. "Come, this is just the beginning!"

We emerged from behind the falls and began climbing upward through a maze of rocks. We were close to the source of the light now. The light traveled through the water, but the source of light sat at the top of the waterfall like a king on a throne. Here was what had caused so much pain to me and everyone I had encountered in the Shadowlands. It was too much to bear. I was now in the presence of the king—this tyrant who had caused all my pain. I stared at the ground.

A voice drifted down from the light. It was not like the shining ones, although the same light alluded from it. The voice was rich and vibrant. He had no defining features—arms, legs, or even a face—just pure light. His presence threatened to overpower me at any moment, even from my hiding place. Yet, he held back.

"Are you thirsty?"

The voice was unnerving. I thrust my shoulders back and set my jaw. However, "very thirsty" was my only reply.

"Come and drink."

"You know I can't," I said, every muscle tensing.

"The water is here for anyone who wants it, but you are right. You cannot drink without first giving up everything."

My eyebrows came together, and, still glaring at the ground in front of me, I shouted, "I *have* given up everything!"

"You have had much taken from you."

"You," I pounded the ground with my fist, "You took everything from me."

"Yet, something taken is not the same as something given. What have you given up?"

"I—" I retraced my journey. I *had* given up everything. My breathing quickened as I searched for examples, but all that came to my mind were the things *I* had taken—not only on this strange journey through this world but in my home. I helped Onn in his attempt to save his world only to get home to my own; I let Avis, Deem, and Magoumi die without lifting a finger, I took Odessa's job for the money; I worked in a nursing home for my advancement; I lied to get a scoop of ice cream. Every selfish thing I had ever done flashed through my mind. Even good deeds I had done in my life were thinly veiled attempts to cover my selfishness. I sat in the dust, appalled by the depths of the darkness in my own heart.

My throat was caked with dirt, my voice was raspy when I finally eked out the words, "Is it worth it?"

The voice softened. "It is worth far more than anything you might give up."

I glanced over my shoulder and slowly rubbed my neck; my other hand hung lifeless by my side, no longer balled into a fist. "How can I know? I keep hearing lies. How can I know if this is true or if I will die and become one of those *things* that are worse than nothing? You gotta give me proof."

"No amount of proof will suffice. You know this. You can only choose to go back or to go forward in faith."

I bowed my head low and traced a line in the dusty ground. "What do you want me to do?"

"Cast off the dark. Step into the light."

I pressed my back against the rock and pulled the cloak tightly across my face. "I have to ask you something."

"It is only by asking that you receive."

I clenched my teeth. "Are you the one they call the tyrant?"

"I am."

"Are—" I shook my head. My whole body was trembling now, "Are you good?"

"That I am. But not what you call goodness."

I clenched my eyes shut, rubbing my temples, "I don't know what you are! Everything is clouded."

"Step into the light so you may see."

I ran my tongue slowly over my lip. I had come planning to tell the tyrant what I thought of him, but now I wasn't so sure. His presence exposed the worst parts of me. Maybe I didn't want to see the truth. We all believe we are the hero in the story of our lives. What happens if we're wrong? *I have nowhere else to turn. Where else can I go from here? The truth, however painful it might be, is in the light.* I tore off the cloak and flung it over the waterfall with one swift motion, and I stepped into the light.

I squeezed my eyes shut and braced myself for the intensity of the unadulterated light. The waterfall's roar sent vibrations through my whole body as if I were in a mosh pit at a concert. Chills rushed over me. I expected to immediately evaporate. Instead, as I stepped forward, all the burning and pain I had accrued was drawn out of me. I took in a deep, full breath and let it out with ease. My shoulders were no longer tense.

The light was absorbing every ounce of stress and pain. I slowly opened my eyes; I wasn't squinting. The world around me looked more beautiful than ever but had no painful side effects. I dropped to my knees, my hands covering my face, as I bowed low to the ground—no longer hiding from the light but instead kneeling in thankfulness and awe.

> The king took the burning upon himself. He is the only one who could.
>
> The flame can't hurt him. He *is* the light.

My every flaw flashed in my mind as the burning sifted away, but the embarrassment, which so often accompanies the acknowledgment of faults, vanished. Now, I was looking directly at the king—without pain. Everything I had determined to accuse him of melted away. Because it was true—entirely true. He was who he claimed to be. He was precisely what every creature, every person, should be but never could be.

How can the imperfect, like myself, ever begin to describe the absolutely perfect? Even the term "perfect" isn't good enough. It gets thrown around in a sarcastic comment or used to describe something as good as it can get, but no one ever encounters true perfection. Whenever I've gotten close to something perfect-ish in the past, it made me jealous. Maybe this jealousy was a small taste of my reaction to true perfection. After all, jealousy is anger at realizing I am not as good as the other guy.

However, when I stood in the perfect light, my imperfections fled like darkness from a flashlight. Instead of jealousy, the king's perfection humbled me. I can only say He is *good* in a way that makes all other goodness, even the most selfless acts of kindness, seem like cheap, goody-two-shoes in comparison. I, too, had been living in darkness my whole life, but now the king took all my flaws, imperfections, and darkness onto himself and destroyed them in his blaze of glory, and now I can *see*.

CHAPTER 39

I STROLLED OUT OF THE THRONE room, a new person. *I'm ready to run a marathon or two.* I stood at the edge of the cliff and surveyed the beautiful kingdom that lay before me. The light was warm and comforting on my skin. The king told me life would not be easy from here on out. He warned me that in some ways, it might be more difficult than anything I had ever faced, which was terrifying because I have encountered some horrific things. Still, he assured me that I didn't have to be afraid when I met troubles because now his light was with me, and I believed him.

"Lindy?"

"Onn!" I spun around, and there he stood. I didn't waste a second; I sprinted toward him and threw myself into his arms. He laughed that same new carefree laugh and spun me around. He was still a shining one, but his light wasn't overpowering. *I must be a shining one now as well.* The light was shining through both of us.

"I—you're dead!" I sputtered. Onn's eyes were the same murky gray.

"I'm so sorry about that," he said, setting me back on my feet. "Are you still hurt?"

"Hurt? Oh!" I had completely forgotten about all my pain, sores, and bruises. I opened and closed my hands with ease and twisted my torso—pulling into a long stretch. "It's all healed!"

Onn's face held that teasing smile I'd always sensed was a part of him.

THE GIRL AND THE STOLEN FIDDLE

"We finished the job," I said, peering up at him, "We finally got it right." The music from the king's orchestra filled the air around us.

"Well, I'm not sure we can claim credit for that," Onn said, "but it is time for me to keep my promise."

His smile faded, and a familiar look of sadness danced in his eyes. It was time for me to go home. Bittersweet excitement washed over me. "How?"

"The Hall of Time. It belongs to the king," Onn started walking through the king's magnificent outdoor palace. I followed him, trying to soak in every drop of this experience. Once again, behind the waterfall, we turned into a different passageway through a stone hallway. Clocks of all imaginable kinds and centuries lined the walls. Each one was set to a unique hour. Onn stopped in front of a jeweled doorway—its colors reminded me of the rainbow that had first brought me into Chaira.

"This is it," Onn said. The jewels cast colorful fragments of light onto his face and skin.

"Where does it lead?" I asked, wondering if I would once again find myself in a blizzard.

"It leads wherever and whenever the king desires to send you," Onn said, looking as if he were just as curious as I was to find out how this worked.

"Come with me." My words came abruptly and without forethought.

He stared through the bright doorframe, lips slightly parted, "I can't," he finally whispered. "My people need to know the truth, and how can they know if I do not tell them?"

Sadness swelled in my chest. "But you said shining ones came to your village your whole life, and you never listened."

"I never understood," Onn said, "but I always listened, and now I understand." He rubbed the back of his neck as he shook his head. "I *have* to try. My Diume and Oi-u, and everyone else. They need to know. I can't leave them in the dark."

I nodded and swallowed back the disappointment. I tried not to think about if I would ever see him again. If I was ever going to leave, I couldn't think about *that*. I stepped forward and turned the doorknob. The other side of the doorframe was nothing but light. Before I took a step forward, Onn reached down and slipped his hand into mine one last time. A single tear rolled down my cheek and landed on the back of his hand. His hand held mine through the dark places, pain, and confusion, and now it was made new, but it was the same hand that had always gripped mine.

Onn held my gaze. "It's time to go."

I drew in a long breath, and then I let go of his hand.

CHAPTER 40

T HE NEXT MOMENT, I FOUND myself standing on the doorstep of my house. I was stunned. In my hand was my backpack, and tacked to the front door was the note I had left there what felt like ages ago. I dropped the bag and stumbled forward, pulling down the note and crumpling it in my hand. I cautiously opened the door and stepped back into my house.

"Melinda! What are you still doing here? You are going to be late to work!" My mom flipped a pancake on the stove.

I ran my tongue over my teeth. "I, I wanted to grab some breakfast."

"Well, you better grab it and go," Mom said, already throwing a plate together for me. I glanced back at the door, and then I ran forward and wrapped my arms around my mom in the biggest bear hug. She was surprised, but she hugged me back.

"Honey, you better hurry. Your Aunt can only cover for you so much."

Then it hit me. *Odessa.*

"Mom, uh, we need to talk, but right now, I gotta go!" I said as I rushed through the kitchen, grabbing my keys.

"Take your breakfast plate!" Mom yelled.

I ran out the door and slid into the driver's seat of my car—not bothering to wait for further protests. Soon, I had hurriedly parked the car in front of the nursing home entrance and charged straight in.

"Melinda, what are you doing here?" My Aunt said as I rushed past, "We've talked about this. I don't want to have to go through this again. I meant it when I said you're fired—"

"I'm so sorry, Aunt Milly, I—there's something I need to do, then I promise I'll go," I said as I rushed forward with only one thing on my mind. My apologetic tone must have left her dumbfounded. She didn't try to stop me, so I whirled around the corner into Mrs. Aidan Odessa's room.

It was empty.

Aunt Milly marched in behind me. "Come on, Melinda. We talked about this yesterday. Please don't make this harder than it has to be."

"Yesterday?" I stared at her in disbelief. "Where is Mrs. Odessa?"

"Oh, honey," Aunt Milly's expression softened, "Mrs. Odessa passed away last night."

"She's—she's dead?"

"She was ready to go, sweety. I've never seen her look so peaceful in all the time she's been here," my aunt said as she moved into the hall. "Go home, sweety."

I was alone. There would be a lot to face when I went home, but right now, I stood motionlessly staring into this room. It was clean and empty. No sign of the fiddle. The sheets were in a pile, ready to be picked up for laundry. The dark curtains that had covered the windows were thrown back, and, for the first time, the room was flooded with light.

THE END

BIBLIOGRAPHY

Oatman, Johnson. "I'm Pressing on The Upward Way (Higher Ground)." *Hymnary.org*, https://hymnary.org/text/im_pressing_on_the_upward_way.